THE
BODY'S PLACE

THE
BODY'S PLACE

ÉLISE TURCOTTE

TRANSLATED BY
SHEILA FISCHMAN

A CORMORANT BOOK

ONTARIO ARTS COUNCIL
CONSEIL DES ARTS DE L'ONTARIO

The publisher gratefully acknowledges the support of the
Canada Council for the Arts and the Ontario Arts Council
for its publishing program. We acknowledge the financial support
of the Government of Canada through the Book Publishing
Industry Development Program (BPIDP) for our publishing activities.

The translation of L'Île de la merci by Sheila Fischman was made possible by a
grant from the Translation Program of the Canada Council for the Arts.

Printed and bound in Canada
First English language edition April 2003

National Library of Canada Cataloguing in Publication

Turcotte, Élise
[Île de la merci. English]
The body's place : a novel / Élise Turcotte ; translated by Sheila Fischman.

Translation of: L'Île de la merci.
ISBN 1-896951-46-5

1. Fischman, Sheila II. Title.

PS8589.U6214313 2002   C843'.54   C2002-905082-0
PQ3919.2.T8714313 2002

Editor: Marc Côté
Cover and text design: Tannice Goddard
Cover image: L'Orpheline by Jean Paul Lemieux,
used by permission of the estate
Printer: Friesens, Altona, Manitoba

Cormorant Books Inc.
62 Rose Avenue, Toronto, Ontario, Canada M4X 1N9
www.cormorantbooks.com

But one day we'll have to put some order into the world;
the heart on the left, the liver on the right,
carefully rinsed in water and vinegar,
like windows.

— DOMINIQUE ROBERT

THE JAIL

It's over, she thinks.

She has put away her school books. Run a damp cloth over every piece of furniture. Now she is looking at her bedroom, satisfied.

Hélène likes things to be finished — a family supper, a month, a year. She likes the worst to be laid out behind her. Today, the worst was extinguished, along with the last hour of the last day of school.

Every piece of furniture, every object in her room represents a part of herself, a clean, smooth section of what is in her soul.

The inside of her body must be like that: a square chamber containing invariable geometric forms. A bed, a chest of drawers, a bookcase. No dirt. Nothing glaring.

She runs her hand over her face, then along the full length of her body.

Is it me? Is it absolutely me?

She goes to the window, opens it, and leans outside to look at the river. After that, she turns her head towards the street.

It's such a small street.

If you look too quickly, you could misjudge and think that it's a street in a nearly dead neighbourhood, frozen in another time. You could imagine that everything is quiet and straightforward there, and filled with normal stories. A young girl could stop in front of the house and shout: Are you ready? Hélène could then hurtle down the stairs, go outside, and hop on her bicycle. But it's not that. Nothing is really joyous, and nothing has died yet. Everything is just a little bit missing, vanished, faded.

Here in the white house on Saint-Réal Street, on the shore of the Rivière des Prairies, close to the island and the railway tracks, not far from the Bordeaux jail either, there is hidden a pain as secret and unexpected as a wedding photo hidden under a big notebook at the back of a locked drawer.

Hélène is fifteen; she is standing at the centre of a perfectly ordered world.

She goes to her desk and checks one more time that her drawer is carefully locked.

It's finished, she thinks again.

A little earlier, along with the rest of the class, Samuel sang a goodbye song to his kindergarten teacher. He pretended to be following, but, in his mind, he was going much faster than the others. He knew that Hélène was waiting for him: she finished school today too. He knew that Lisa would be the last to come home and that the house would finally belong to the three of them. He saw the summer unfolding exactly like the previous one: alone at last, between his two sisters, in a kind of kingdom.

"Come and read my book," he says.

He races up the stairs and holds out his book at arm's length to Hélène.

He pleads: "Come on, Lène, come and read the book."

Hélène half-emerges from her reverie, then looks at her little brother: it's going to be an ordinary day after all. She sits on the stairs and opens the book for the thousandth time.

"They live in the forest," she begins.

Slowly she closes the book and runs her hand over her face again.

"I don't feel like reading, Samuel."

He starts to whine.

Then Hélène makes a huge effort to overcome the irritation that sweeps over her again.

Why always the same book? she whispers.

She makes one more effort to bring back the image of her perfectly tidy room, then she tells Samuel: "Okay. We'll start again. They live in the forest. Most of them have yellow eyes . . . That one is a great grey owl."

She gets to the end of the book, then Samuel leaves her alone on the stairs.

There, that's finished.

In fact, it's not finished at all. The afternoon hasn't even started. Hélène counts the hours as they pass. She wears a huge watch with phosphorescent numbers that she can't help looking at all the time.

Samuel often thinks about the hours, too. He constantly asks what time it is.

We have to follow a timetable, Samuel always says.

It's the strongest tie that connects them, him and his oldest sister.

Lisa behaves differently. She thinks that the raison d'être for each thing has no need of external signs. For example, she says that the raison d'être of time always lights us from inside.

Lisa, age thirteen, crosses the street with her head so high it's as if she wants to disappear into the sky. She comes drifting back from her friend Florence's because of the free time now spreading out before her. Her first year of high school was difficult, every day bearing down on her with its full weight though she's usually so expert at escaping from reality.

She goes inside and flops down in her favourite chair. Hélène looks at her, shrugging: her sister must have been adopted.

"Much too happy," she hisses between her lips.

"Still," says Lisa, "I'm going to miss my teacher."

That's the stupidest thing Hélène has heard today. Except, of course, for each of the sentences spoken by Claudia, her own teacher, as they were leaving. All the others had already left the class, but the teacher went on talking to her. She said she suspected that Hélène sometimes needed help. Hélène for her part was thinking about someone holding her by the arm. It's a kind of love, Lisa would surely have said. Love. A force that always holds us by the arm. But Hélène wouldn't talk to Lisa about it. Her friends had left without saying goodbye. Two minutes later, Hélène didn't give a damn.

"Let's go to the park," says Samuel.

"No way," replies Hélène.

All three are sitting on the big sofa in front of the television and have no inspiration. Nothing that can make them inhabit the present moment.

Hélène knows that it will be like this every day of this interminable summer unless she reacts. She has to make a decision, but she still can't do so. Unlike her sister, who is busy brushing her long brown hair, she can't focus her attention on some precise thing. She sees her mother going out again, then coming back to the house a little more tired. She sees her losing her temper, changing her clothes, or pacing the living room. As for her father, he can spend hours doing calculations on the dining room table. After that, he'll station himself at the window. These are precise moments resulting from certain decisions. For her though, everything outside her body seems different, detached, as if such things are part of another reality. She would like to do something, perform some action that would let her enter into that reality. Lose her temper, for instance. Every time, someone holds her back by the arm. Every time, her anger keeps advancing, but Hélène stays behind.

"Okay. The inside of my body is a room and everything in that room is clear and in its own place."

Hélène repeats that litany as she gets up, while Samuel looks at her, stunned.

"Where are you going?"

"I have to phone mom."

The time has come. She looks at her watch and scowls as if she's just done something forbidden. Slowly she punches in the number, slowly enough to repeat to herself each of the words

she's preparing to utter. But as soon as the phone starts to ring, she suddenly has nothing to say. Always, that terrifying impression of never having anything to say! She knows that it's incredibly irritating to her mother. Why call me if you haven't got anything to say? she'll ask again.

She's right, why not keep quiet?

But it's too late, her mother's voice is already there at the other end, and Hélène can't be silent. She panics.

"Samuel broke the blue glass plate."

"Well then, pick up the pieces!"

Hélène hangs up and goes back to the living room. She thinks for a moment, then she takes the blue glass plate off the table, beside Lisa's feet, and throws it against the wall. After that, she goes to get the whisk broom and bends down to pick up the pieces.

"What'll I do with the pieces?"

"Put them in a box," says Lisa. "We'll try to glue them back together."

Hélène turns to Samuel.

"I said you did it, but it doesn't matter."

She takes him in her arms to reassure him. He breaks away and pushes her.

Head down, he leaves the living room with Lisa.

Now Hélène is there alone with her transgression.

I'm a mean person.

All at once there's a whirlwind in the room inside her body. Mean, she says. The word appears to her then as a little ball of solid material. She rolls it between her hands. She goes up to her room, opens the window, flings that foreign body into the air, the wind, the leaves.

"I wanted to tell her I'm not staying here all summer."

She says that as if it were a new and different litany, an idea she has to believe in.

"I wanted to tell her not to count on me to look after Samuel again all summer."

But the words break away from each other and she sends them flying out the window too.

⚜

So routine. An uneasiness that's hesitant, improbable, but so routine. Hélène is sure of it: even Lisa will realize it some day. Even Samuel. Even the walls of the house, the furniture, the rungs of the chairs. Even the neighbours, if it weren't their own suffering, to which they have not yet lent an ear.

She shuts the front door behind her, then goes into the living room. It's late; she walked along the river for a long time.

She stares at her parents, settled on the sofa. Seeing her, Samuel runs to her, shouting: "Lène, come and see my castle!"

He pulls her by the arm to the place where the treasure is. Lisa is smiling. Samuel grabs his dragon and howls as he runs around his castle made of blocks.

"Some peace and quiet, please!" begs Viviane.

She stands, then sits down again, a little farther from her husband.

Hélène looks at them again.

They're married, she thinks.

It's a very small thought, hard to believe, that goes through her mind. They are married. It really did happen: she in a white dress, he in a white shirt, a midnight blue jacket with a bow tie. They must have looked like the other people who got married that day.

7

The thought that's hard to believe unfurls slowly until Hélène's father demands in turn: "Children, quiet, please!"

Lisa falls silent. Samuel keeps up his racket. So they're sent out of the living room.

Not Hélène, though. And even if they did chase her out she would stay there as long as she wanted!

She studies her mother's legs, then her father's arms. Their hair: her mother's, curly, thick as a mass of caramel that doesn't seem to be where it belongs, and her father's, short, thin, already mostly grey. No spectacular beauty or ugliness, nothing distinct, aside from the way that their faces go tense whenever they're next to one another.

Is he going to smile? Hélène wonders.

She focuses on her father's mouth.

Is he going to smile and make some remark? Surely not.

Viviane moves first. Stands up. And Robert just stays there under his cloud of words; as usual, they haven't had time to form a sentence.

He sighs.

Hélène also sighs.

Her mother is breathing elsewhere in the kitchen. She lights her cigarette. She senses her will gradually weakening.

She looks up at Hélène, who has joined her.

"What are you doing here?"

"What about you, what are you doing?"

Hélène waits for the reply. Then Viviane tells her: "I hate this kind of conversation and you know it."

"What kind of conversation, mom?"

Hélène feels like pounding her fist on the table. School's been out for a week already and not one word has been uttered in this house, not one word that has been truly sensed, real and significant. Aside of course from Samuel's squealing, from Lisa's furtive remarks.

She wants to so badly. Wants to find out what connects two individuals like Viviane and Robert. To be able to imagine them completely outside herself, arguing, jostling each other in the kitchen; two bodies, well defined in the light, filled with words and joined by a visible thread, no matter how tenuous.

But that thread disappeared long ago.

A fundamental tie has disappeared, Hélène knows it. And without that tie, without that natural quality that gives shape to all the other qualities, there is nothing more to hope for. Until a fist, no matter which one, finally comes smashing onto the table.

⚜

Lisa, Hélène, Samuel listen at the doors.

Saturday morning: all three are outside the parents' bedroom.

"What're they doing?" asks Lisa.

"You know perfectly well, they aren't doing anything," replies Hélène in her coldest voice.

If Lisa thinks they're doing what she imagines they're doing!

"They never touch each other."

"They aren't even whispering," says Lisa.

"They never whisper in their bedroom, just in the kitchen."

"They're sleeping," says Samuel.

"That's right," says Hélène, "they're sleeping."

"How come we never go on vacation?" asks Lisa.

Hélène looks at her sister, surprised: here she is finally asking a question. She stuffs a piece of brioche in her mouth, then makes a face as she swallows it.

"And how come we haven't got many friends?"

Their father, finally up, has planned a family breakfast. A pleasant one. A pleasant family breakfast and Lisa's pleasant little questions.

"Because you don't want any," replies Viviane.

"Maybe you're too happy here, just the three of you," tries Robert.

"No. They don't want any."

And so that's that for Lisa's question. And so that's that for Samuel, who starts making faces, too.

"What do you mean, no one wants any?"

"Because we don't know how," says Hélène.

And that's that for the pleasant family breakfast.

Later, Hélène lies on her bed drawing squares in the air with her fingers. Her eyes are closed. She is methodically filing her family memories.

She starts with the wedding, which for her is not a memory but a hypothesis. Such a strange idea. So atrociously happy.

Yet there they are, from the back, in the chapel with its panelling. They turn around right after their mutual consent. They cast delighted looks all around. After that they get into their car to celebrate with their friends.

And then I was born, already brilliant, a big girl with golden hair.

And what do you know, now it's Lisa's turn.

So there they are, the two girls in the tub. Both standing, nearly twins, wrapped in a big yellow towel. Here they are in the park, here they are at school. Hélène, the first, and right after her,

Lisa, so perfect in everybody's eyes. Lisa, delicate, defenceless; the opposite of Hélène. And there we go! Something disappears and there we go! Back it comes.

And then, much later, it's Samuel's turn.

Hélène remembers how much she loved him! At the age of ten, so worried when he cried in his cradle. Worried and furious when Robert and Viviane quarrel. When they fight over Samuel's ridiculous tiny pyjamas.

And all at once: a vacuum, sucking the house into a whirlwind of silence.

Poor Samuel, thinks Hélène. Poor Lisa, who's never understood very well. Poor house, full of deceptions and mistakes.

She opens her eyes and stands up, to put an end to her little game.

"Not again!" she exclaims as she walks into the living room.

Viviane is on her feet, holding some toys. Her face is closed. Fenced in. She's complaining about the house. Samuel is watching television, his little hands over his ears.

Hélène remembers what her mother told her one day: "Stop crying if you don't know why."

She looks at her mother and repeats: "Stop crying if you don't know why."

Viviane looks up and replies: "But I'm not crying!"

"You should be," Hélène tells her.

She takes Samuel.

"Come with me, I'm going to hypnotize you."

"What about Lisa?"

"She already is."

"And mummy?"

"Yes," says Hélène. "I'll hypnotize her too."

"And daddy?"

With her mother, the confrontation is constant and laden with innuendo. Before, a kind of mystery emanated from her body. Now, when Hélène looks at her she can't even tell if she's pretty, if pretty is a suitable word for a woman like her.

Viviane's like that: absent, separate from others. It happened little by little, and little by little Hélène could no longer find an adjective to describe her mother.

As for her father. He has been conquered by the outside world.

Hélène imagines him in his computer store. He talks to his customers in the confident tone that he sometimes uses on the telephone. Another man, almost.

Good for him, she firmly believes.

A kick at the wall.

Good for all the others.

"I'm not going to just stand there and let something happen."

Hélène says this to Lisa, who is suddenly all excited. The world is a vast, threatening territory, but they won't let themselves be had.

"So what exactly are you going to do?"

"Whatever. Exactly."

She opens her bedroom window wide and starts to yell.

"That's just one example," she says when she has finished.

A very mediocre example. For the time being, she knows, her own will never takes her far enough, is never powerful enough to get her away from here.

She shuts the window again and her mother appears, out of breath, at the top of the stairs.

"How can you yell like that?"

"With my lungs."

"You know what I mean. Why do you yell like that?"

"Because I'm scared."

"I'm scared," repeats Viviane, imitating her daughter.

"Of you, you scare me," Hélène continues, as if she hasn't heard.

Silence.

The bedroom could explode and no one, not even Lisa, would be surprised.

Hélène imagines the pieces of her own body scattered across the room. Her mother's forming a single column, lined up carefully against the wall. Her brother and her sister still alive, dazed.

She wrings her hands; it mustn't happen here, in front of them.

She tries to push aside the power that forces her constantly to imagine scenes like this.

Lisa and Samuel aren't involved in this; above all, nothing must happen in front of them.

But of course nothing explodes. Nothing ever explodes. And the world is still threatening. And the lie, so obvious.

⚜

Will it go on like this forever? Hélène asks the question of her hands, her eyes, her feet. Will we walk in the same direction for a long time to come, cross Bois-de-Boulogne Avenue, Desenclaves Street, wait for Lisa outside Florence's house, push Samuel in the swing? Will we go on seeing things that don't exist, go on being the target of people who don't exist?

Hélène looks at her feet, which are moving forward, and tries to locate the moment when the menace began. She can't do it. Things never begin exactly at the moment when they begin. Her mother's smile, for instance, when did it really begin to disappear? When Samuel was born? Surely not. Hélène sees again her mother singing softly to him all the time. She seemed so happy to have had this baby. A tiny little boy. Robert seemed happy, too. They took turns looking after him and some days, if the weather was fine, they would take him to Raimbault Park where they'd stay for hours. Hélène could add still more virtues to the ones that the two of them formed. So it wasn't that moment that made her mother's smile disappear.

Maybe it happened a little later, on the day when she said she was leaving for good. Hélène only remembers Samuel's cries. And Lisa, sprawled on her bed, so calmly leafing through her book of stickers. Lisa, who never says anything. Lisa, who plays at being someone who doesn't exist.

But maybe her mother's smile disappeared long before that day, long before it was erased from her face. In any case — and Hélène is sure of this — it was no longer there on the day when she came back.

Her father left too, and he should never have come back either. Afterwards, they tried to erase their inability to understand. But it's everywhere around them. Like their sacrifice. They claimed to have come back for them, for the children. But they should have simply left them to their own devices, there in the white house. They should have left them to some other form of sadness, grave but precise. That's it, they should have left them to a precise sadness instead of bringing back with them an uneasiness so vague that they could say nothing about it, a hidden and frightening uneasiness like the rumble of thunder or, even worse, the imminent overflowing of the river.

Now they are motionless.

Mute.

Except when a moment of fury passes through Viviane's eyes. Then she leaps to her feet and gets ready to give instructions. She mutters as she fixes her hair. You, Hélène, and you too, Lisa. You're old enough now to tidy your own rooms. Old enough to keep an eye on Samuel. To stay by yourselves, shut up in the house full of locks. Old enough to know what it means to walk in the darkness of the island, to hear the spring break-up, to watch out for padded footsteps creeping up behind you.

Life is a constant danger.

And so the menace may have also started long before. Maybe it has been inscribed forever, along with fear, in Hélène's body.

Her body.

She thinks about it now as if it were a limit to the universe. The world is delimited, in part, inside a body, hers. She does her best to see it as part of the outside: trees, houses, Hélène's body. A bird, a cat with sticky fur, a man pushing a baby carriage through the park, and Hélène's body. Who else thinks about that body as being a part of the outside? No girl, no boy in her class: for them, as for Lisa and Samuel, she is merely an extension of what's inside. She belongs to her class, to the house, to the brain. She belongs to feelings. Or to the absence of feelings. She is never fully an other. Never foreign enough.

But here in the street?

The body circumscribes the menace and it is in the body that shame begins. She looks at her feet. And what if they were to stop moving forward? She walks into Nicolas-Viel Park. Abruptly takes a seat on a bench.

Make me be nobody. Make everything stop and make me disappear.

☙

Life is a constant danger.

Viviane has just repeated that to her children again. They're sitting in front of the TV set watching the news. Except for Samuel, who is still playing with his castle.

"The world is sick," says Viviane.

"You're the one that's sick," retorts Hélène.

"What do you mean, I'm sick?"

"Never mind."

"No way. This time I do mind."

"Stop," murmurs Lisa.

"Now what is it?" asks Robert.

He gets up to turn off the TV and deal with this question.

But it's too late, another moment of rage has just passed.

Then Hélène goes up to her room with Lisa and as soon as they've shut the door, they burst out laughing. They enumerate all the warnings their mother has given them. The times when she has pointed out people to whom some dreadful catastrophe has happened. Neighbours. Cousins. Even her own friends. All those people sucked in by death despite themselves. Sometimes by the most violent acts. They must never go too far away. Take yesterday as evidence of danger: a missing notice has gone up all over the surrounding area. A girl your age, Viviane was quick to say. Just fifteen. Maybe a kidnapping. Maybe a runaway. Naturally a disaster.

"A tragedy," repeat Lisa and Hélène, laughing.

They laugh like two little girls, without limits. They collapse under their own laughter. Under the house that is falling apart. Under the ruins. Under the vast, black, wordless unknown.

What about Samuel? Suddenly Hélène stops laughing. She tears down the stairs, grabs Samuel away from the inertia that must never, ever overcome him.

"It's time for the owls. Come on, Samuel."

"Are we going to read?"

"We're going to read."

He gets up and follows Hélène.

They call Lisa to come and join them. Then all three leave the house.

Viviane and Robert watch them go, unable to move.

Summer night. Silence.

They stay there, together. Alone, and separate. A little more lost. In their white house on the river.

Two

SHAME

"Are you sure?" asked Lisa for the third time.

"Absolutely," replied Hélène.

She has pulled on her jeans, drawn a fine black line around her eyes.

"It's your turn to stay home."

Several days went by before she told them of her decision. She's well aware that all the stability here rests on her shoulders. She herself is so afraid of disorder, so afraid of what shifting a single element in so fragile a group can bring about. But it's a question of survival, she told Lisa.

"What about me? How will I manage?"

"You?"

"Yes, me. And what about Samuel?"

"I don't want to think about that."

Hélène must have really hypnotized Viviane, because after a short time she gave her agreement.

"In a garage!" she had exclaimed at first.

As if it were unthinkable for her own meticulous and tidy daughter to spend her days in such a place — dirty, masculine, and so far from what she thought to be her universe.

But finally she shook her caramel-coloured head, saying that maybe it was a good idea after all.

"A very good idea," Robert confirmed that evening.

In any case, they had no choice. Hélène had already given her answer.

And so every morning Hélène gets up and goes to work. She opens the door, a breach is formed, the outside world penetrates into the house.

There she is, leaving to go to a place where no one knows her. A place where sentences don't bounce off the walls, where she has to stay on her feet in the sun, or in the rain if it's raining, and repeat formulas that are polite, necessary, useful, that have nothing to do with what she's feeling. For she feels practically nothing, only the impression that she's a surprising girl who knows how to do a few things in a space full of intoxicating smells.

Starting now, I'm nobody, she thinks as she walks.

It's already so hot today that she has to take an elastic from her pocket and pull her brown hair into a ponytail. She knows that it makes her look even younger, but it doesn't matter. Why do girls her age always want to look older? She checks her clothes and tries hard to get a complete picture of herself. But it's not possible. It has never been possible. She thinks back to her attempts to go out with friends. A movie, the bus, the basements of numerous houses . . . Every time, it ended in disaster. The others: they fill the space so well with their bodies, their movements, their words. While she, even if she just wants to have some fun, has to work at it so zealously. Though she tries to have a clear vision of what's going on, to keep her eyes open so she won't be snatched up by the music, to be solidly present, everything invariably comes apart into pieces of oneself, pieces of incomprehensible language, pieces of herself.

It's because I'm not normal, she thinks.

And so at this very moment she feels the weight of her footsteps when she turns onto Bois-de-Boulogne Avenue. Her steps, like each of her actions, still seem fabricated to her.

She stops briefly in front of the boxing club's windows, gets a glimpse of her own reflection in a kind of mist, then continues on her way, crosses two more streets and finally spots the sign for Émile Letellier's garage. She walks into the shop.

Behind the counter, Huguette smiles at her.

"I've been waiting for you."

Hélène looks at her watch, then sighs with relief: she's on time. Exactly on time.

Huguette starts to laugh.

She pours herself a mug of coffee and as she does every morning, signals to Hélène to take a seat beside her.

Hélène enjoys this moment, even if she's still a little uncomfortable. Huguette is so different from any other people she's known so far.

A short time ago, she and Émile bought this old garage and moved back to the place of their childhood.

"All I wanted was to have some peace," says Huguette.

To have some peace. She tells about how many times they left

21

everything behind to have some peace. They've travelled, run an inn on the St. Lawrence, then came back to fix up this old garage.

"Time to get to work, Hélène," she says now, pointing to a car that has just pulled up to the pump.

Small changes pad along in Hélène's mind. She is somewhere other than inside herself, for once. She is living someone else's life.

The customer smiles at her. She says good morning, unscrews the cover of the gas tank and inserts the nozzle to fill it up with gas. It's an absolutely perfect smell. Surprising. She closes her eyes so she can capture it properly. She can sense the approach of the moment when she'll have to open her eyes.

She breathes in the smell. Here, she has nothing to protect. Not herself. Not the others.

From a distance she sees Huguette busy at the cash register, a smile still on her lips.

Émile spends his days repairing cars in the shop at the back. Hélène admires his determined movements. So intense and resolute.

Movements, smells, words: everything quickly becomes a stage set for Hélène.

She moves around in that stage set. She's someone else. Until she goes back to the house.

Hélène has the feeling that she now lives a double life. Both of them real.

In one life, everything is guilty. Everything demands a reaction.

In the other, light and perfect moments exist, because there is nothing and no one to protect.

In Hélène's absence, Lisa has to stay inside the house as much as possible. Florence comes to spend a few afternoons with her. They help Viviane fix dinner, then they settle onto a big blanket in the yard, in the sun. Very soon, Florence will be going away to live for a year on the North Shore. They talk about nothing else. Viviane repeats her orders, but the girls don't listen: they're lying in the sun, no hats, no sunscreen, no shade. Too bad for them, Viviane catches herself thinking as she observes them through the window.

Viviane is on vacation and in two weeks it will be Robert's turn. It's been a long time since they've wanted to take their holidays at the same time. This way is more practical, they tell the children when they ask why.

Today, though, Hélène isn't there to play with Samuel, to talk to him, take him to the park, and for Viviane, having to spend the whole day here with her own indifference is nearly horrible.

Samuel does his best to attract her attention. He hovers around her with his book about owls. After a few minutes he gives up and goes to his room. He starts drawing monsters. He works frenetically. Now and then he stops to listen to himself talk.

"When will Lène be here?" he asks Lisa, who's getting ready to go out with Florence.

"Don't bug me," she replies, moving away.

She comes back a moment later.

She plants kisses all over his adorable little face.

She leaves again.

He stays there, waiting for Hélène.

It's nothing.

It's not a school day. It's not exactly like a summer day. It's not sad. Not even a beginning of sadness yet.

Exalted: that's the word that is making Hélène drag herself along the road home. She thinks: "I have to be exalted."

She pictures her classmates who dash in every so often with news of some overwhelming event. The suicide of an idol last April, or a simple change that's occurred in their minds. So many stories that never touch her. She remembers reading these words in the paper: died of a shotgun blast to the head. These words had fascinated her, only the words, and she'd pasted the article into her scrapbook along with other headlines.

Lisa and Florence are often exalted too. Sometimes Hélène sees them dancing and howling songs. Those of the dead idol, for instance. Then they sit down, all out of breath, they huddle together and whisper secrets.

Even Huguette and Émile look exalted. Hélène has never seen two people smile and embrace so many times in a single day. She looks at them until she can't stand it any more, then turns her head away abruptly.

I ought to feel some intense emotion, she thinks.

Finally get out of this house.

Meet new people.

Think for a fraction of a second that her family is behind her and dead, never to be alive again, never again to be part of her.

But on the way home she drags her feet and doesn't feel any emotion that she considers strong enough. Aside from the strange happiness at smelling on herself the smell of gasoline. She moves from one world to another the way the gasoline flows through the hose. That's all. Her body would sometimes like to faint on the sidewalk. Her hand would like to brandish a weapon and silence all her enemies. Her muscles would like to be filled with determination like those she sometimes spies behind the windows of the boxing club. But she keeps moving on and life continues to flow through her limbs, her viscera, her guts.

I won't say anything.

She comes home again with the certainty that she must say nothing about her day. Those moments may be empty, but they're hers.

I won't tell them anything.

But no one asks.

Except Samuel, of course.

She opens the door, shouting: "Come here, Samuel, I'll tell you how Émile fixes motors."

But Samuel isn't there and neither is Lisa or Viviane.

Hélène sits on the front steps, at a loss, her head in her hands.

"Where are they?"

Where are they! When just five minutes ago she wanted them all to disappear!

This is inexplicable, she thinks.

This is totally obscure.

But she stays there, nodding her head, for seconds, for minutes, for a whole hour, until they come home.

"Where were you?" she asks.

"At the park," replies Viviane, surprised by the severe tone of her daughter's voice.

"What about Lisa? Where's Lisa?"

"At Florence's, probably."

Hélène looks at Samuel: he seems tired. Dirty and tired.

"Lisa was supposed to be looking after Samuel," says Hélène. "Not you."

She takes her little brother away to give him a bath. Viviane follows her up the stairs.

"What's got into you?"

"Since when do you take Samuel to the park?"

Viviane turns around and goes back downstairs. She doesn't want to answer. She sits in the kitchen and as she does at this time every day, she feels sweat running down her forehead.

Robert will be here soon. She'll have to find ways to avoid talking to him, even looking at him. Nothing that Hélène does, nothing that she says, nothing that sometimes spatters her stony gaze — none of that then can touch Viviane.

They all eat at the same table, outside, on the deck.

Lisa has put on the cloth and set the table with cutlery, glasses, even a bunch of wildflowers that she picked near the railway track.

Sometimes Lisa seems so proud of what she does, so confident; as if she's feeling an intense joy that takes her away and then separates her from her body.

It happened not five minutes ago, and now she still seems all shaken.

"You look out of it," Hélène tells her.

"What d'you mean, out of it?"

"You've got that mystical look."

"So what!"

"That's enough!"

Robert has spoken.

They eat in silence for a moment that's too long for Lisa. Back on earth again, she asks her father why she can't have in-line skates.

"Your mother thinks they're too dangerous," he replies.

"She's right," says Hélène, "if you get on a bike or put on skates or walk on the sidewalk, there's a good chance that you'll die."

She stands up and adds, raising her voice: "Most of all, if somebody touches you, you die."

Now Robert gets up.

"That's enough, Hélène."

He grabs her by the arm and drags her into the kitchen.

He tries to talk to her. He wants to understand, to get to the bottom of something for once.

But Hélène retreats inside herself and refuses to talk to him.

She goes up to her room, sits at her desk, waits for the anger to pass.

Very quickly it passes, with a shrug.

Life fluctuates like that between Hélène's two worlds.

One day, Claudia comes to the garage to get gas.

She sticks her head out her car window and recognizes Hélène.

She seems genuinely glad to see her. Delighted. Surprised.

But Hélène doesn't react: she'd have given anything for Claudia not to have seen her. Her former teachers stands there in front of her; Hélène listens to her while she watches the numbers on the meter.

Then she looks Claudia squarely in the eyes: "Things are going fantastically well!"

Claudia turns her head away for several seconds. Finally, she bursts out laughing.

"Terrific!"

She drives away, a smile frozen on her lips.

After her comes Florence's mother. And Monsieur Valenti, who lives next door on Saint-Réal Street. Both of them surprised to see Hélène working at the garage. Both of them with a question.

Hélène furiously wipes her hands on her jeans: all that's missing now is a visit from her parents. How could she have thought that her two lives would never cross?

At the end of the day she goes to the shop at the back where Émile works. Right now, it's the place she likes best, the one that the inside of her body should start to resemble. Everything is in order there, like in her room, except that here, disorder is an accepted idea.

Back home, she goes up to her room and opens the drawer of her desk, where lie the wedding photo and the notebook that, for months now, she hasn't allowed herself to open. Hélène has drawn up her own list of regulations. Not to open her notebook any more. Not to confide in anyone. And above all, not to let in too much information. At once she locks the drawer, then lies on her bed to think about Émile's moves, about his big hands that operate so elegantly inside the bellies of the cars.

Now, whenever Hélène gets the chance, she sits near him to watch him work. She observes him as she pleases: he concentrates so hard that nothing disturbs him. She tries sometimes to guess his age. She wonders if he could be interested in her. When that thought goes through her, she shudders, immediately overtaken by shame. She thinks about Huguette, and her shame branches out. How can I want him to be interested in me! she chides herself.

It happens to her more and more often: Hélène is afraid that her thoughts will become desires. If she takes Samuel for a walk, if the fear of losing him grabs hold of her, she ends up believing that it's what she wants. The same thing sometimes if a customer looks insistently at her when she's bent over the windshield. The same thing for fifty scenarios that pass through her, soundlessly, like heat lightning in the sky.

She shuts her eyes, then opens them again. She breaks the image of her thoughts and comes back to the surface again.

She looks at her own hands.

She too must get around to controlling everything.

Bordeaux is a cramped neighbourhood. Here, persons, the names of persons, their sentences, go back an infinite number of times to the same place — a tide that wears away the most solid rocks. Hélène must get used to the idea; it's inevitable, most of the garage's regular customers soon call her by name. She's no longer an outsider. Some talk about the weather. Others tell her something about their lives. She smiles at them without replying.

It's lunch time.

She eats in the shop with Huguette and Émile, watching for the next customer to arrive.

José shows up, a regular: he brings news about Marie-Pierre Sauvé, the young girl who has disappeared.

The neighbourhood is small. The circles surrounding Hélène are small, and that's how she comes to believe quite naturally that something is pursuing her. There's no doubt about it, her two lives are connected.

There's a newsstand in the shop, visible enough for the horrors to be displayed in front of everybody, but Huguette and Émile don't read the papers. Neither does Hélène. Another of her rules.

She wishes she could avoid even glancing at them. She was barely interested in the Missing Child notice that her mother showed her, to scare her. She doesn't think about it any more. But as soon as José started to talk, she looked up at him: his words found an echo in her.

She looks at him, stupefied: that thing is pursuing her. It's an event already lodged inside her like a gene, in a sense, and it will always be so and she won't be able to do anything about it.

"I thought it was finished," she says.

She regrets immediately having made this remark out loud.

Suddenly she's annoyed, irritated, as if some invisible being has her glued to the spot, keeping her from getting up and going on with her work.

She has to put some order into her ideas, but José doesn't stop talking.

He follows her when she goes to his car to fill it up, and he doesn't stop talking.

He just dropped the news like an overly heavy package, and now the contents of the package are spilling out while he talks about this and that and Hélène does her best to put some order into her ideas.

She tries not to think about the details she'll discover if she ever decides to open the newspaper.

Not right away.

She sees herself on the street, in her neighbourhood. She sees that street, deserted, and at the end of the street the railway track crossing the island filled with legends where the body of a fifteen-year-old girl has just been found.

It's insane. Unexpected.

Though Émile and Huguette pay no attention to what José told them, every customer who comes to the garage today has his own idea about the tragedy. It happened so close to where they live. Why here? Didn't their island already have a rather questionable past? Why in their neighbourhood, which is already marked by death, boredom, prison, and not where the victim came from?

Hélène doesn't listen. Most of the customers don't speak to her anyway. She must not listen. It's pointless to know that another murder has been added to the series. Pointless to look at the photo of a young girl who was missing and believed dead, then try to see the same photo now she is known to be dead. Pointless.

She goes on working, deaf to the rumour that keeps growing around her.

At the end of the day, she folds the paper under her arm and takes it home.

She cuts out the articles, opens the locked drawer, hesitates briefly about breaking her own rule, then decides to take out the scrapbook.

She turns the pages one by one.

Then she pastes these new articles after the others.

This time it's different, she thinks.

She gently closes the drawer.

From her window, she looks at the river; it's so close that its odour surprises her sometimes in summer, when the wind brings it into her room.

The island is just next door.

She has lived here all her life, amid the odour of trees, of thawing earth, of dirty water and dead leaves. There is a street,

Saint-Réal, but here, on the cul-de-sac, you smell mainly the river. And now?

Now it's happened, thinks Hélène. No one wished for it. No one could have foreseen it. It happened, that's all.

It's a fact. The earth has spun on its axis, the young girl was suffocated as she cried out, and it really did happen.

๛

Hélène sweeps the floor of her room. Then she sweeps the kitchen floor, giving a gentle push to Samuel's feet as he follows her everywhere.

She knows what is sleeping in her locked drawer and she must perform a series of precise and orderly gestures to keep herself from going back to her obsession.

Two lives, Hélène orders.

No *idée fixe*, no obsessive fears, she begs silently. And she sweeps the dining room floor, then the living room.

And what if it were me?

She stands in front of the mirror at the front door.

And how far will my thoughts take me now?

At six o'clock, while Lisa, all alone in the yard, is taking tiny sips of juice, Hélène is feeding Samuel. Viviane isn't home yet. From where? Hélène doesn't know.

"Did mummy go out to sell houses?" asks Samuel.

"No, no," she replies. "She's still on vacation."

"If at least she drank," mutters Hélène as she studies the contents of the refrigerator. She, and her husband too, why not? If at least they had a passion for something, even a simple bottle of whatever.

32

Hélène winces. She suddenly sees again the mother of one of her friends, on the night of a party, begging her to brush her hair. She was moaning. She seemed so confused that Hélène couldn't refuse. But she didn't want Hélène to stop. She held onto her arm firmly, she talked, sometimes interrupting herself to sip some beer. Then, in the middle of the night, Hélène and her friend had found the woman passed out on the bathroom floor.

Hélène briskly shuts the refrigerator door.

She just wants her mother to come home.

She looks at Samuel. He is methodically eating everything on his plate. How can he always be so docile?

"Are you happy?" she asks him.

"Why?"

Sitting on his chair at the end of the table, he waits patiently to know why he should be happy. But Hélène can't think of anything to say. She rinses his plate, then calls to Lisa, but Lisa is concentrating so hard on the juice coming up through her straw that she doesn't hear her.

"Lisa never wants to eat with us," says Samuel.

"What do you mean?"

"She stays in her room."

He shrugs.

"No, I'm not happy."

"Why?"

"'Cause there isn't enough Hélène."

He smiles. His remark has had quite an effect on his big sister: he knew what he was doing.

"We're going to play!" he orders.

"Okay. Till mom comes home," says Hélène.

She takes a deep breath. She hopes that her mother won't talk about the murder of Marie-Pierre Sauvé. She hopes that there aren't any stabs to be delivered with the help of the perfect conditional. That she won't say the word "safe." You see, Hélène, outside we aren't safe from anything. As if they are here!

And then, no. Her mother comes home and doesn't talk to her about anything.

She's gone shopping and she sets bags full of clothes at their feet.

Hélène would like to congratulate her. The words she holds back are tickling her lips. She's strong though and she manages to let out only some inconsequential words.

All she has to do now is jump into her father's arms when he too comes home and it will be the resumption of a very clever comedy.

It's the family comedy.

Hélène thanks her mother for the flowered dress she's just bought for her. She's the oldest, she has to set an example and make the first move. But what she'd like to say is that she hates flowers.

She doesn't, though; her mother already knows it. She puts on the dress in front of her and that means: See how I resemble you? A lie. Exactly what her mother wanted to hear.

Then Robert comes home. Hélène greets him by jumping into his arms.

"Look at my new dress, dad!"

He's nearly bowled over. His arms stay stuck at his sides.

Then Lisa and Samuel throw themselves into the game the

same way you throw yourself into the amusement park when the gate opens. They understand perfectly well the meaning of this comedy; it's short-term protection.

They take turns trying on the clothes and it's Lisa who finally wins the best actress prize: a real fashion model, so thin, so deceptively obedient.

Hélène applauds. What's floating around her is the power of lapsed concentration. She knows that she's been successful, for this evening, in diverting the current. She has stopped the rise of impetuous waves, she has pushed them back because a family is a family, because flowers are flowers, because a murder is a murder.

A little later, she carries Samuel up to bed when Lisa finds him asleep on the sofa.

She'd like to bid her parents goodnight before she goes up to her room. She'd like to put on flowered pyjamas, get into bed and fall asleep thinking about the goodness that sometimes emanates quite simply from the order of things. But that's asking for much too much. A comedy's a comedy and she won't go that far.

She kisses Samuel and strokes his hair for a while.

She leaves Robert and Viviane alone in the living room, or on the deck, wherever. Let them do what they want, let them be silent as usual, or let them unfold plans and believe adamantly that they're going to renovate their house. It doesn't matter. Let them stand there with their arms stuck to their sides!

She lies down on her bed with all her clothes on; she deliberately keeps her eyes open. Now she can linger over the description of the body of Marie-Pierre Sauvé.

At the age of fifteen, strangled, hair plastered down and full of twigs, she must seem smaller. So small that the body gets to the point of resembling a rock perhaps, or a piece of clothing left behind in the woods at the beginning of winter; a bright spot in the middle of the forest.

But this is not a forest, it's an island. And the spot must smell musty because when all's said and done, the girl had been dead for quite a long time. Maybe she'd been locked in a shed before she was moved into the open air. A small spot that for a long time was nowhere to be found. Now unrecognizable.

Unrecognizable, that's what has fascinated Hélène since the beginning of her obsession. A specific number of days, blood and air, and soon the body is unrecognizable. Already it's no longer her, Marie-Pierre Sauvé, but it still is her, precisely. You realize that very quickly if a piece of clothing is found near the body.

At the edge of the woods, or on an island, after days of searching, identification is sometimes possible only because of some unfortunate and, at first glance, insignificant detail.

This time, the article says, the orthopaedic prosthesis and the clothing have confirmed what they'd been dreading since yesterday.

Hélène studies these words without comprehending. What had they been dreading? Why is it worse that it should be her and not someone else?

And if you plunge deep enough into these words, if you open them, dissect them the way a cadaver is dissected, will you finally know at what precise moment the body lost its identity, at what moment the voice stopped crying out?

Hélène hears Marie-Pierre Sauvé's cry. It passes through the silence and echoes off the walls of the house.

Is that the moment when the blood congeals in the body? Does it thicken, stopping the air and the outside world from coming in?

&

To understand words, stop them from emptying themselves: that's what Hélène calls studying. She studied till she heard her mother's footsteps on the stairs. She hasn't retained any images, images don't interest her. She has fallen asleep and hasn't dreamed. She's too ashamed to dream.

Twice she got up to check that Samuel was asleep. She even glanced into Lisa's room. She is afraid that the contents of the words will spread to them and that they'll catch them, like a disease.

That's why, in the morning, she stays in the shower for so long.

Lisa knocks on the door.

Then Viviane.

"Hélène, hurry up! I'm going back to work this morning."

It's Robert's turn to stay home.

In fact, he's already downstairs, slightly uncomfortable; he scrutinizes Samuel's face, trying to detect a glimmer of affection.

Scrutinizing faces is something that Hélène, too, has often done. For so long she spied on her parents in search of a particle of a reason to live. Time and again she has sat in the kitchen, waiting for one of the two to make a move towards the other. That waiting is now something in the past.

"Hélène, get out of the shower!"

But why is her mother in such a hurry? After all, Hélène thinks, she's the one who taught her to be so clean. She's always said that you had to be clean before anything else. To be ready for anything that might crop up. Because you never know. Anything can happen, without warning. One day or another someone might come too close, lean across, sense desire. Even if it doesn't exist. Even if it has never existed. And anyone at all can sniff fear.

Viviane knocks on the door again.

"Hélène, what did I tell you!"

But Hélène is washing. She's scrubbing her skin with what Samuel calls a towel-mitt. She's trying not to think about Marie-Pierre Sauvé. So close to her. So close to the house where everything is clean, where no one knows what it feels like to die. When you really suffer.

Hélène is washing herself: her mother mustn't come into the bathroom and sniff her fear. And Robert mustn't catch Viviane knocking so hard on the door.

"Hélène, will you get out of there!"

But Hélène still doesn't come out.

Only Samuel could make her leave the bathroom. And as chance would have it, he's climbing the stairs right now. He wants to know what all the noise is about. No one answers him; he tugs at Viviane's dressing gown and she, too exasperated to restrain herself, finally takes out her exasperation on him.

Of course. That's what happens in any family. Everyone is so generous. Each person takes on so naturally the nervousness, the sorrow, the anger of the others. And there you go: making Samuel cry was all it took to get a reaction from Hélène.

She dashes out of the shower.

Lisa rushes into her room.

Robert sprints up the stairs and arrives just in time to hear Hélène tell her mother: "Touch him again and I'll kill you."

But Viviane hasn't struck Samuel, she just yelled at him for no reason.

Robert is tearing his hair out.

Hélène is fulminating. In any case, someone in this house will have to die!

Night, day, garage, house. An obstacle. And now there is a stir in Hélène's body.

⚜

It was a pleasure for Hélène to make that statement. Touch him again and I'll kill you. It was easy, much easier than protecting Samuel from the silence, from the nothingness, from the threat that is like nothing else.

"If you go away I'll jump down," Samuel said after that from the top of the stairs.

But Hélène left anyway. Viviane went back to selling houses. Robert stayed on a chair in the kitchen. And Lisa. Lisa put her pillow over her head; she wanted to stay out of everything.

"Île aux Fesses is where my parents kissed for the first time," says Hélène. It's where everyone went to make out, whence its nickname.

"All right, that's enough," insists Huguette.

José is there already, summing up the news.

"Haven't you got anything else to do?" Huguette asks him.

But José plainly never has anything else to do. He's a big boy of thirty who still lives with his parents, who looks after his car as if it were a pet, and who peddles news.

"Apparently she was strangled to death," he says.

"Strangulation and cranial trauma," Hélène points out.

She has studied well. So well that the words emerge from her mouth with no emotion.

Huguette doesn't seem to care for this. She looks at José as if he's just committed some grave sin.

"Are you sick or what?"

Then she motioned to him to get out of her sight.

"Are you afraid?" she asked Hélène a little later.

"No more than usual."

Hélène stares at a black stain at the bottom of her T-shirt. She suddenly feels very tired. Huguette asks too many questions.

At the end of the day, Hélène walks home, constantly turning around.

A body that was mutilated, then lost in the neighbourhood.

Her mother says: "Always look behind you."

The policeman says: "Don't walk alone at night, don't light any fires."

The newspaper says: "Life is monstrous behind you, ahead of you, and around you."

⚜

Hélène stops outside the boxing club. She steps up to it, looks in the windows.

Inside, two boys are training.

She has the impression that as soon as they spot her they step up their efforts. She thinks that their movements are then directed at her. Their strained muscles. She has a nearly irresistible urge to join them, to pull on gloves and fight with them.

Why am I alive?

She raps once on the window.

Why her and not me?

She raps again.

The boys stop, surprised.

Hélène runs away as fast as her feet will carry her.

Be careful, don't light any fires.

She runs all the way to the house.

She wants just one thing: to go up to her room as quickly as she can, open her desk drawer with the gold-coloured key, to finish with the contents of her scrapbook.

An hour later, she writes this: There is a tie between three of the seven murders: the victims are lying on their stomachs, naked, their neatly folded clothes beside them.

Neatly folded clothes.

The murderer rapes the girl and folds her clothes.

Sophie Laporte, age 11, strangled, a black T-shirt next to her body.

Émilie Côté, age 17, blows to the head, a blue T-shirt, a red sweatshirt.

Marie-Pierre Sauvé, age 15, a black jacket, a black T-shirt with Converse on the front.

Hélène closes her notebook.

Sometimes the body is in a state of putrefaction too advanced to determine if the murderer raped the victim.

This time, certainly, she thinks. Certainly.

She shuts the drawer and jumps up, shakes her head: that vision has to go, it has to go, it mustn't even come into the world.

Three

THE ISLAND

*B*ut things come back. Even if they do not come fully into the world, they do come back.

In 1974, when Viviane and Robert kissed for the first time, they had to take a very narrow path along the railway track to get to the island on the Parc de la Merci, which had long been known as Île aux Fesses. A path sometimes strewn with dead leaves and empty cigarette packages, with crumpled papers and other signs of human presence. Even though it was a wild spot where not many people came.

This evening, a July evening in 1994, Hélène isn't sure about taking the little bridge which for several years now has made it possible to cross the river totally confident, totally clean, some-times on foot, sometimes on bicycle, because a bike path joins up with it too: a sign of the existence of human beings who've become concerned about the quality of their lives in this place now marked by fear and disgust and only yesterday ringed by a security perimeter. Though the papers insist that the murder wasn't committed on the island, still no one feels like walking there, or sitting in the sun, unwrapping a sandwich and opening a beer to celebrate the arrival of summer. No one feels like snuggling up to the loved one who might be lying close by, to kiss that person on the face, the neck, the hair, the sun-warmed arms, no one feels like pressing hard against someone with his powerful weight. Everyone is under duress.

That's what Hélène thinks, facing the island alone while doing her best, once again, in vain, to imagine how her father's tongue was able to enter her mother's mouth, how his arms could have wrapped themselves around her, and the rest, yes, the rest. How, for anyone at all, could she imagine all the rest?

But twenty years ago the story of Viviane and Robert was perhaps, was surely, more innocent, more lucid, more fluid than a single word spoken by one of them today.

In 1974, five years before Hélène was born, her father's tongue had perhaps quite fluidly entered the mouth of her mother, Viviane, the girl he'd been desiring for some time now and with whom, like so many others, he sometimes took evening walks on this island.

Viviane was twenty-four. She still lived with her parents on Notre-Dame-des-Anges Street. Robert, with two or sometimes three roommates, shared a big apartment on Bois-de-Boulogne Avenue. Hélène knows all this. She knows her mother liked going there; she liked to sit on the big wine-red velvet sofa and let herself be overwhelmed by the free and easy manner that prevailed around her. And so, Hélène supposes, shortly after the first kiss she would have liked sleeping with Robert in his always unmade bed, getting up in the morning in a cloud of indolence, of limp and disorderly ideas. In her, life must already have been so rigid, and so friable.

Robert is a gentle man: the way he'd kissed Viviane that first time on the island was different from anything she'd experienced before. She had decided that evening Robert was the one her fear could lean on. Love had to have been a kind of wall that fear, memory, even the future could collide with and then be modified. For of course most things can only be lightly modified, not altogether transformed, not denatured.

The island, for instance.

Maybe it's in the nature of the island to harbour corpses.

Now that a young girl's body has been found there, for the time being — in the eyes of a certain number of people in the neighbourhood — it is no longer anything but a theatre open to dreams and to cruelty. Memories, which are often suspended from the trees or encrusted in their bark or, like those of Robert and Viviane, lurking under a rock, are also, unwittingly, touched by this event.

On that island though, beneath the layer of memories and well-kept secrets, who knows how many rapes and even murders have been committed there?

Even though the papers repeat: it wasn't there that Marie-Pierre Sauvé was raped and killed.

There, in the least-visited part of the island, under a tree at the very edge of the river, in the early summer mud, she was only hidden or, rather, deposited.

Of course.

Because even though everything is clean here in 1994, it's still a place that is naturally favourable to camouflaging a dead body. Naturally haunted by the notion that something dirty could happen there.

For that matter, every day, here or elsewhere, it happens.

In 1974, thinks Hélène, maybe the island was just as poorly kept up as her parents have described it, littered with trash, but her mother's kiss was without a doubt clean, absolutely clean, even if it was liquid.

Her mother described the kiss to her and Lisa in detail one day when they were picnicking on the island, with Samuel asleep in his stroller. And then what? Hélène never stops wondering. And then? Because Viviane has never revealed the real details.

And Hélène has never given a kiss. She's sure that she's the only person in the world of her age who has never given a kiss. She has always escaped just in time. Just in time from the island too, just in time from the schoolyard, the street, the park, across from the corner store, the bus stop, and so forth.

Order: do not let the tongue, the spit, the germs of another person enter your body.

But one day — it's happened to everyone, it's already happened to nearly all the girls in her class — it will have to happen to her. She'll have to agree and move her body towards it. And the rest, yes, the rest of the gestures of human, of animal instinct, which Hélène has not yet experienced but which caused her to be born. She'll have to say yes. Even if it would be simpler to be forced. Obliged to do it. Here on the island, for instance. It would be better to plunge all at once into humiliation, to keep her eyes open and that's that, the deed is done once and for all and let's not say another word about it.

Nadia, the first girl in her class to have done it, had closed her eyes and opened them again right afterwards: in front of the bathroom mirror, alone at last, she had looked for a mark, for some sign or other of the change that had occurred in her life. But all that she'd found was a slight colouring in her cheeks, like after a volleyball match at school. A little difference that hours later was completely gone.

But nothing is ever really forgotten, thinks Hélène on the bridge to the island.

Memories sometimes come back at the most unexpected moment. The sad hair of her friend's mother comes back. The bodies of all the Marie-Pierre Sauvés come back to the island. Fear, objects, clothing, the customers at the garage: every day they come back. The photos in the newspaper, on posters. The words in her notebook. The bad dreams. Everything comes back. Even her parents' first kiss; it comes back — a troubled soul in the water of the river.

Hélène hesitates again before plunging into the island. It's been dark for too long already. If her mother finds out that she's come here she'll have a fit. She'll kill me, thinks Hélène. Viviane must be so afraid at this moment, at this time of the evening, when there is so much cruelty and her oldest daughter hasn't come home yet.

But Hélène has to go there.

All those who've gone before her have of course combed the island thoroughly in search of a clue. But now maybe she will see and comprehend what everyone else has missed.

José mentioned it this morning: a phone line has been set up for anyone with information to provide. She may use it and give someone one millionth of an answer. As if a millionth of a retrospective thought inside her could provide the key to what really happened. What even the autopsy can't reveal. What was killed first, for instance. The words she uttered. The name she cried out. As if some part of her was the part to which it had already happened. One millionth of a prospective thought. Hadn't her mother often told her, long before this event, never to go to the island at night, and above all, never alone? This is what will happen to you. You see, it happened to young Marie-Pierre Sauvé.

So she goes there.

⚱

There's no one; Hélène can hear her heart beating. The blood rises to her head.

You'd think that the island had been deserted following a war or an epidemic.

Since the corpse was discovered, even though the security perimeter has been lifted, the island seems to have been abandoned by visitors, forgotten by the cry that must have been heard, that must have echoed this far but was lost in the sky, between rows of houses, or in a concrete corridor, or under a wood floor, a carpet stained with blood.

For she must have cried out the name of a person, Hélène is sure of it.

At the moment when she knew that she could do nothing more, Marie-Pierre Sauvé must have been surprised to hear herself crying out that name, a last-minute revelation. Maybe it was her boyfriend's, or her father's. Or maybe she could only moan a very faint, "Please," as she knelt before the deepest, darkest precipice ever created by man. That's a formula Hélène has often heard at school. The most diabolical invention ever created by man. Anyone can fall to their knees one day, beg for mercy, moan a tiny, an insane, "Please," before the enormity of the cruelty. Anyone who can cling fast to life and haul out a prayer from their very depths.

That is why, thinks Hélène, a name always bursts into the brain at that moment. You close your eyes so as not to see anything, so as to disappear, to escape from pain, and that's how the deluge appears: a stream of known words and landscapes that fall into the brain out of nowhere. And at the end, a single name. If it happened to her it's Samuel she would think of, first and last. It's with the word "Samuel" that she would pray for it to stop. Samuel would be the name that would cascade into her head.

That's how she could be bound to life.

But she is alone: no one behind her, no one ahead of her. No angel of death comes to clutch at her neck.

And if she goes on walking like this, with so many thoughts, Hélène will have to lie down on the grass, here, or else cross the railway tracks that divide the island in two and go down into the wildest part, right at the water's edge, at the very place where the body was found, and stop there and start to cry.

But it would be pointless.

Even if everything that comes back did come back.

Her tears would enter the earth and, as the days passed, join the river.

And it would be totally pointless.

A sorrow with no reason for existing.

That's why she starts to run, bumps into a tree, then another, and runs and crosses the bridge, dripping with sweat because it's so hot, and runs some more on the street even though there's no

danger for her, precisely because it is that, the shadow of her death, that is following her, her fear transmuted into desire. She runs inside the house, and warns her father who leaps to his feet when he catches sight of her: "Don't say a word."

Same thing to her mother. There. Because it's an absolute certainty: she doesn't want to hear a word from them. Not tonight. Not them. Or anyone.

But that turns out to be a kind of incoherence too, a flaw in reasoning, because it had barely occurred to her, alone on the island, that she never listens to anyone. Even if the others around her — her mother, her father, Lisa, Claudia, Émile, Huguette, José — seem to believe very firmly, during at least an hour of their lives, in the immanence of their own presence, in truth there is never anyone.

Otherwise, why would such disorder, generated by a single cry, be possible?

Four

THE BODY

"This time she's gone too far!"

Viviane is categorical: going out after dusk is out of the question. Her words have already made the rounds of the house and the garden. No one knows yet if it's a punishment or not. No one knows exactly what has gone too far.

Robert doesn't agree.

"We certainly aren't going to lock her up!"

But Viviane has made up her mind and as soon as Hélène heads for the door, she grabs her arm.

Hélène starts to mutter: "One of these days I'm going to leave for good."

"If you go, I'm going too," said her mother.

"What?"

"If you go, so do I."

"But you aren't me," Hélène exclaims. "You aren't me!"

She glances at her father, hoping he'll step in firmly for once. Then she shuts her eyes and plunges once again, alone, into the island.

She can't believe it.

She shouts: "You aren't me!"

She'd like to grab her mother by the shoulders and shake that crazy idea out of her head and onto the floor. She sees herself squashing that idea the way you squash an insect: by pressing very hard on the carapace till a whitish liquid spurts out.

A cracking.

She'd like to hear the cracking of the carapace of all the ideas that are spreading around her. She stamps on housing prices, which are in free fall. She stamps on the unemployment rate, the latest models of computers, pollution, violence, and the new rash of murders. She stamps on youth, environmental protection, prevention, recycling, respect, survival.

She'd also like to slow down her own momentum.

But nothing stops.

And now, to everyone's surprise, Lisa comes hurtling down the stairs, shouting that she can't take any more fighting. Amazed by the sound of her own voice, she falls silent, then starts to cry.

And now Robert too is getting worked up. He raises his voice: "This is unbearable."

And it all combines to form one tangle of intertwined threads of anger, of unsaid words, that will pass once again through the living room and touch Samuel's living space. And if Hélène goes away he won't be able to live. Not for the time being and in particular, not here.

Now it's his turn to start howling.

He is there, in the eye of the storm, and what he has understood is that Hélène is going away.

This time he could quite simply threaten to kill himself. Coming from the mouth of such a little boy, such a peaceful child, "I'll kill myself," would perhaps have the effect of a bomb that would silence them all forever. After all, "I'll kill myself," is a remark he's often heard from Hélène and even, but only once, from Lisa.

But words have no impact here. What Hélène says, what Viviane and Robert don't say, Lisa's mysteries — all that is stagnating in the house like the toxins in the river.

"I'm going to murder somebody," says Hélène.

She goes to Samuel, picks him up and whispers that she'll never leave him all alone. The thought of her little brother all alone is one that she'll never be able to squash completely.

"See you later," she tells him, still whispering.

She looks at Lisa, helpless, totally silent again.

And despite her mother's ban, and though she's following her around and threatening her with a thousand punishments if she opens that door, Hélène opens that door, then slams it as hard as she can.

Hélène is a tall girl, strong, human, and the door slammed so brutally that all at once the tumult inside the house has stopped.

Of course. Once again she's the one who has triggered everything.

Samuel's sadness, Lisa's confinement to her room, the end of the lovely comedy, the lovely lunch, the wonderful supper full of silent ecstasies: she's always the one who triggers the crises.

How could her mother guess that she'd gone for a walk on the island? Hélène can't comprehend. Her mother must be crazy, too.

Otherwise how could she imagine the murder and the blood inside the mind of her fifteen-year-old daughter? How could she imagine her fascination and at the same time her disgust?

But the fault is only Hélène's. If only she hadn't started working at the garage. If she'd stayed home to take care of Samuel. To keep Lisa company.

Marie-Pierre Sauvé was certainly guilty, too, when she left her house. Or maybe only furious: she walked too fast and took a false step, just one false step that caused her to stumble, then fall into the trap. Or maybe the false step was already inscribed in her. Didn't Hélène hear a teacher of self-defence explaining on television that most assault victims are already in a state of weakness: they have the gait of a victim. The movements and the body of a victim. So she was guilty, or sad, or totally despondent, but not enraged. Marie-Pierre Sauvé was walking with her head down, brooding over something, as Hélène is now, that's why the man noticed her and that's why she fell into the trap. If she had been enraged, she'd have fought, she would have torn the man to pieces and transported the body to the Parc de la Merci.

It's insane: Marie-Pierre Sauvé had simply left her house to go to her girlfriend's. And Hélène doesn't want to believe what the self-defence teacher said. There's no reason. There must not, there cannot be an explanation. That would be even worse.

Who can know what happens — and why it happens — between the moment when a girl walks out of her house, smiling and wearing new clothes to go to a party with her friends, or quite simply to buy some bread, or to run away from home in anger, and the moment when she's found dead and naked on the shore of a river, or buried under a pile of garbage, or carved up at the bottom of a quarry.

Carved. Hélène stops and squashes that word.

She didn't want to think of it ever again.

She'd always thought that it could only be used for the bodies of animals. But she had read it, it was there in the newspaper in black and white. In the first article she'd cut out.

How is it possible? How can you say "carved" for a human being? Hélène had wondered furiously.

But she'd read it in the paper. It was real. Someone had done it. Someone had said it, then written it. And she herself, as perverse as the others, had cut out the article and stuck it in a scrapbook.

Now she is walking along a street, in a city, in a world where the possibility of such words is suspended, and she doesn't really know where to go. Certainly not to the island, not this time. She's already so guilty. So secretly guilty.

And so furious.

"Why does she hang around on that island?" asks her stupefied mother, vaguely sickened, of the kitchen counter, the ashtray, the window above the sink.

"Why not go to your girlfriends' instead?" said her father, as he's been saying all year.

But Hélène has never wanted to have real friends. Every time she's got close to someone, that tie has finally become a burden to her.

She is walking down Bois-de-Boulogne Avenue towards the garage.

What would Émile and Huguette say if she threw herself into their arms, begging them to let her spend the night with them?

What would they say if she smashed a window, if she broke

in and slept on the floor?

They would find her there the next morning, and then they'd take her to their house. It would be immediate, irrevocable: no kitchen with objects flying around, no witness, no whispering. They'd take her in and that would be that. They'd kidnap her. And then they'd kidnap Samuel. And Lisa.

&

How to know if you're a victim? Hélène wonders again. Eyes glued to the sidewalk.

Thinking: I am guilty.

Until the moment when she stops, looks up to realize that her steps have brought her to the former fire station that now houses the boxing club.

Each thing, each being has its destiny, her sister Lisa always says. And what if the destiny of her escape tonight were to stop here, go inside, bluntly expose herself to an assault?

Hélène has only been here once before and she's never forgotten it. She was with her father, who knew the trainer and had gone in to say hello. They'd talked for a long time while she sat on a sofa and watched the boxers training. A sensation had swept over her, so confused that there were no words to describe it.

"What are they doing?" she'd asked her father.

In a secretive way, she was trying to find out what it was that she'd liked, certain that deep down she wasn't allowed.

Robert hadn't answered.

Tonight, though, she is alone at the window.

She sees two boys in the ring and at the back of the room, two others working at the punching bag.

Someone is sitting at the desk. She recognizes the trainer.

The ring. Hélène had never noticed how worn the ropes are: they're all frayed. The boxers' feet are dancing crazily, the frayed ropes are swaying, and it's like the moment when the wind blows through a house in ruins.

As far as Hélène is concerned, they're lucky they fight with their fists. She is certain they have perfect control over their bodies. On an evening like this one, damp, without direction, they're already at the centre of the heat. A war could break out, the heart of their anger could burst, but they would be ready, they would be there, already inside the action, bodies straining to dodge, at the hub of the danger.

The boys must be around twenty: that's enough for her to feel attracted by them. She could pick one and he could rescue her with his muscles.

She contents herself with watching.

She is so absorbed in their movements that she forgets what has driven her here, why she is guilty and should throw herself at the feet of the first person who comes along and beg forgiveness.

Then the round is over.

The boys catch their breath.

She catches her breath too, and though they haven't waved her in, that won't keep her out. There's an old beige sofa resting against the wall, the same one she sat on four years ago; if it's still there, it's surely in order to tell her to come in, sit down, catch her breath too. Like anyone else. Like a little sister who comes running inside to admire her tremendous brother training there. As she has nothing else to do, as she has no one, she could certainly transform herself into a little sister for a few moments and stop being the cause of the overflow of misunderstanding that submerges the house.

So she opens the door as confidently as if she's done it hundreds of times. She walks around the ring and flops onto the old sofa.

The trainer gets up to urge on the boys who are launching into a new round.

"Move!" he orders one of them.

Then he goes up to Hélène, he seems to recognize her and asks if she's Robert's daughter.

"What can I do for you?" he asks then.

"I just want to watch," Hélène replies. So sure. Apparently so sure of herself.

He shrugs impatiently and waves his hand: she can stay.

Anyway, there was no question of her leaving. Nothing could make her leave. She wants to sit and watch. Wait. Breathe. And there's nothing to add.

It's so clear, so obvious that no one here seems to take offence.

Hélène is now a little sister, sitting on the sofa like a good girl. She keeps staring at the boxers' feet. Behind her, as in any other club, the walls are hung with old fight posters. She feels a constant vibration throughout the room. Or maybe it's inside her body.

What came over me?

She can't move. Even if she wanted to get up and leave, she couldn't. The impulse that's lurking in the room has just nailed her to the sofa.

She is sitting and watching two boys who are boxing, so close to their bodies she can pick up an odour that's so ambiguous, so strange. The moves she could make, that she can feel stirring in her but holds back, probably all originate in the same flaw and could take her outside herself. A long way from everyone's picture of her. Those moves would make her disappear.

I'm fifteen years old and I'm sitting here to make a choice, she thinks.

See how I too am starving.

Her gaze lights then on the bodies, and after that it climbs slowly towards the faces.

The boxer whom the trainer ordered to move seems filled with the severest tension. She stops at him.

But very quickly she has to close her eyes, suddenly gripped by nausea because of the stifling heat, getting worse and worse, because of the blood that could spout — she's seen that in a movie — from one of the two faces that, as she has carefully observed, are straining with the effort. They're making a terrible effort. Why? wonders Hélène. Why that effort, and why don't they look at her, why don't they direct that tremendous effort of all their muscles at her?

What got into me? she asks herself again as she tries to open her eyes and get up.

But she can't, her eyes are hopelessly closed, her limbs paralyzed; she can't think about anything except the sweaty shorts sticking to the boys' skin, about their muscles, their thighs, their arms, and about the frayed ropes, about the threads that hang down and dance to the rhythm of their feet.

Shame, blood, tumult.

What would happen if one of them approached her?

She'd just be getting what she deserves. Or so she thinks, in there, even if she knows that it's the most sordid thing she could think about.

"Be careful, you're a girl," Viviane and Robert told her one day, in unison.

"It's normal to feel embarrassed when men look at you," Viviane added as if she were stating the obvious.

But it's her own gaze that embarrasses her. An embarrassment like what she feels at this moment: intolerable, complete, unfair.

It's over.

The boys emerge from the shower and dry their hair. The one she's chosen has his eyes focused on her.

It must be late: everything seems quiet on Bois-de-Boulogne. Hélène has had so many visions before the light goes out in her head. She is waiting now for a tide to sweep her away.

The trainer stares at her as if to say that he's sorry he has to send her away.

"Say hello to your father for me."

The boy comes up and sits beside her.

Here is my destiny, thinks Hélène.

"D'you like boxing?" he asks, somewhat mocking.

"Maybe," she replies.

He can see her confusion, but he doesn't try to understand. He smiles. The possibilities of his strength scatter around him.

They stay like that, talking for a moment.

Then he asks where she lives and offers to walk her home.

It's Robert who is waiting on the gallery for Hélène.

When he sees her coming along with Martin, he rushes inside.

He has decided there won't be any more squabbles tonight.

Hélène stands there, silent, not sure how to react. She thanks Martin quickly and rushes inside in turn.

At once, Robert orders her to apologize to her mother. In the interests of peace, he's prepared to do anything, even to hide Martin's existence from his wife.

Viviane listens to the lies of her daughter, already sunk into indifference again.

Then Hélène goes upstairs and kisses Samuel. He's asleep, a prisoner of his dreams.

Lisa is spending the night at Florence's, who's going away tomorrow.

Poor Lisa, thinks Hélène, she's going to be even more alone. Poor Samuel.

She gets into bed and punches away at her pity.

She has to think about Martin, about Martin's smiling mouth, about Martin's body. She has made the decision. It's him, it can only be him. And she has to be ready for the very first time.

⚜

Two days a month, Hélène stuffs herself with aspirin so she won't feel her belly being torn.

It's one of those mornings.

She gets up grumbling, pulls the sheets off her bed to put them in the laundry, carefully chooses what to wear. Nothing must show. That's another form of threat and she will again spend the day looking behind her.

You're a girl, look behind you.

Hélène is always afraid of losing or forgetting something. Even more these days.

All girls experience this fear, she thinks, as if it were an absolute principle. They get up and look behind them to see if they've left anything on the seat in school, on the subway, in the park: a bag, glasses, a glove, part of their body, why not? A particle of oneself, an odour, a stain everyone can see. Or an object that will stay there and can't be found, an earring fallen to the bottom of the river, disappeared into oblivion. To get up, take a step, then turn around to check if there's a bloodstain behind — she's certainly not the only one who does that.

She swallows her first two aspirins.

This body — how to stop it, how to be sure of mastering it?

A passing weakness, she assures herself at the mirror.

This evening, everything will be back to normal; she'll return to the club and see Martin again. She dreamed about it all night and now nothing could make her change her mind.

She'll take Samuel. That will be easier.

Hundreds of calls have been made to the phone number provided by the police, but nothing has changed. The murderer is still at large in the city, still alive and free. Hélène imagines him having an instant coffee in the morning when an image may pass before his eyes: the supplication on the face of Marie-Pierre Sauvé.

Impossible not to think about it because posters were put up all over the neighbourhood this morning, to find the murderer. The same thing in Villeray, where she came from. The smiling face of Marie-Pierre Sauvé appears on brick walls, on tree trunks, inside public buildings. Underneath her smile, the amount of the reward, like in a western.

Though Hélène walks with her head down, it's the first thing she notices. The photo. She doesn't understand why they always use the same one. The same smile. The same dress indicating that the photo was taken at some special event. Maybe on her birthday. Whatever it was, Marie-Pierre Sauvé was smiling. And it was a genuine smile. Now that she's dead she's still smiling, at every street corner.

Hélène actually thinks that the posters have been put up just for her. She feels as if she's following a trail that could well become hers.

At the garage, they've started talking about the murder again. They feel sorry for the parents who've just been given the body of their child.

Hélène waits till her lunch break to read the paper. She notes the date and the time of the funeral. She learns that the friends of Marie-Pierre Sauvé will soon be able to pay her a final tribute. The ceremony will take place at her school. She clips the article and puts it in her pocket.

Another paper also shows a photo of two of her classmates. A boy and a girl. Hélène looks closely at the photo. The boy in particular. No one has said anything yet about Marie-Pierre Sauvé's boyfriend. What if that were him in the photo, the boy she thought about just before she died? If only she, Hélène, could be interested in boys her age, like the others! But if such a horror were to happen to her now, she wouldn't have a name in mind to cry to for help, no boyfriend's, not even her father's.

She clips that article too.

The day passes slowly, like a sleepless night.

Late that afternoon, Émile comes to get Hélène and show her how to change tires and fix flats.

She listens to the instructions. She removes the worn tire, rolls it to the back of the shop, then replaces it with a new one.

She looks at Émile, smiling.

Hélène has the impression that her dream isn't over. There's a little sweat on her face.

First Martin's body, then that of Marie-Pierre Sauvé's boyfriend, and now the hands, the words of Émile.

Her dream has stolen part of the day from her.

♔

Hélène has to lie to her parents so she can take Samuel; Lisa refused outright to help her find a pretext. She racks her brains for a moment, then comes up with the lie.

Immediately, Lisa exclaims that she doesn't want to stay here on her own.

"What difference does it make if we're here or not?" asks Hélène. "You're always shut up in your room anyway!"

And that is when the train really starts to go off the track. Hélène stares at her sister as if another Lisa has just appeared. A Lisa who has come down to earth and is now suffocating in her cell. A Lisa who finally can't take any more pretending.

But it's the same Lisa who has thought things over and who finally says: "Okay for tonight."

"What are you going to do?" insists Hélène.

For the first time, her sister appears to her as a complex person, maybe as unstable as she is herself.

"Write to Florence," Lisa replies.

"But she just left!"

"Exactly."

"What do you mean, exactly?"

"It's an exercise."

That was Lisa all right! An exercise! Hélène can go in peace, she knows that her sister will be spending the evening writing her letter. At least she won't be taking part in the drama of the empty space that's being played out in the living room. Lisa always tries to find the most significant way to do a deed, no matter what it is. If reasons are to light us from inside, she has said, you have to practise letting them come to the surface. The meaning of writing a letter will quietly come to the surface in Lisa, then take her once again as far as possible from the here and now.

Samuel is holding his big sister's hand, so excited that he keeps asking her the same question.

"We're going to the boxing club," Hélène tells him. "But you mustn't say."

"Where we go, Lène?"

"To the boxing club, Samuel."

"Where?"

"To the boxing club. It's a secret."

Hélène thinks he understands; he knows from whom the secret must be kept, otherwise he would have already asked why it was secret. Samuel's favourite word, after "hour" and "owl," is "why." Even if there's no question, in Samuel's mind there is always a why.

Why is it a boxing club? he could very well ask.

Why is he Martin?

Which comes down to wondering why things are what they are. Why aren't they different?

The house: why is this one his and not another?

The parents?

The street?

The school?

Samuel, like Hélène and Lisa, is always walking on slippery ground.

He lets go of his sister's hand when she opens the door of the former fire station. He stays behind her when she goes up to Martin, who is pounding away at the punching bag like a maniac.

I know just what I'm going to do, Hélène told Samuel before they went inside.

But she doesn't know anything.

She smiles at Martin, who barely looks at her. Even worse, he goes on punching the bag and looks rather annoyed.

Then Hélène turns around sharply to Samuel.

It's nothing, she tries to think.

Nothing.

She had thought that he'd be expecting her. It was a fantasy she'd believed in: he would wait for her. He, too, had a kind of need and that's why he was punching an opponent and why he was letting himself be punched in turn. It's also why he was waiting for her to come back to the club so that they could try, later on, to create together a moment of redemption. But that's a stupid story.

Girls my age are always dreaming about stupid stories like that, thinks Hélène. She opened the door to the club and no one was expecting her. There's no one: that remark brought her here, it will make her leave again. It's a crushing fact; no one can get to the bottom of himself and grasp the difference, the disorder within order. And outside this place, Martin does not exist. It's all alone, absolutely alone in a totally limited sphere of action, that he is correcting a particle of the universe.

Hélène would like to leave, but Samuel starts hovering around

Martin. Martin stops to talk to him. Finally, Hélène and Samuel have permission to sit and watch him train.

There's no one: that thought continues to pass through Hélène. Then she starts to transform herself.

A sudden urge to go farther, to act in such a way that Martin is under some obligation to her. At first, physically. And then.

And then?

To know everything, right now. It has nothing to do with love. Nothing to do with her parents on the island, the wedding in the chapel, the transformation of the walls of the house into walls of ice. To know everything in a single first time.

She gets up, approaches Martin, asks if she can try.

"Look. I'm going to wear gloves too," she tells Samuel.

She pulls them on.

"Imagine you're facing up to somebody," says Martin.

"Go on, Lène!" cries Samuel.

Right away she starts whacking the punching bag, seeing herself as her own enemy.

⚜

Several times she goes back to the club without Samuel.

"What do you want?" Martin finally asks her.

"What do you mean, what do I want?"

Hélène's hands start to tremble.

"You can't come here every night."

Hélène feels again an enormous weight in her chest; she can't think of anything to say. The air is full of worn-out words that circle above her like falcons circling their prey.

"I haven't got anything else to do," she says.

She looks at the posters on the wall. She looks at her feet.

Then she looks Martin squarely in the eyes.

"I don't know what to do," Hélène repeats.

"That's not my problem," says Martin. "I come here to train, not to look after some little girl."

Why did he say that? How can he be so angry? Hélène doesn't understand. She hasn't done anything, said anything, she just delivered a few awkward punches to that stupid bag of sand.

He said: some little girl.

He's angry. Like her mother whenever Hélène disturbs her though she seems to be dead in the kitchen. She shouts. Her father merely chews the insides of his cheeks. Only once, he went further and struck. There's still a mark — a simple mark, nothing obvious — on the wall. But the other blows, those of her mother, her father, her own, are still in the air, as worn-out words are here. Like Martin's breathing, his panting, still lingering around her.

"I didn't ask you for anything," says Hélène.

Get up. Leave. Above all, don't turn around.

Outside, though, Martin follows her, driven by some constraint or, even more, by some kind of appetite. His footsteps ring out behind her. She runs. Her own footsteps are so soft that they seem to melt on the pavement.

Follow me, be angry. That way it'll be perfect: you force me and I force you.

He grabs her gently by the arm.

"Come on, I'll take you home."

She frees herself with a movement that's far too brusque, because he was barely holding on to her.

"Cut it out," he ordered.

It makes no sense. He knows it's unrealistic, he could simply go away; she knows it too, but he keeps walking behind her until the moment when she stops to show him the photo of Marie-Pierre Sauvé in the window of a grocery store.

"Apparently they've put up eighteen thousand."

"What?"

"But what difference does it make?" she adds, as if she didn't hear Martin's question. "What difference does it make? She'll still be dead. She'll still be dead anyway."

With that she turns and walks away, leaving him alone and baffled on Gouin Boulevard.

This time, she knew what to say.

She's smiling now, certain she has stamped her presence on Martin's mind and body.

Five

WILL

*E*very time she leaves her neighbourhood, Hélène feels she is running after danger. It's a stupid, uncontrollable fear. Not even a fear, a thought, just the beginning of an idea, but it's real, and it's from that reality that the danger comes. Danger of losing herself. Of being left to herself.

Which is why, following the example of her parents, who are always warning her and Lisa, Hélène doesn't often leave Bordeaux.

All the girls her age rush at the slightest opportunity to escape from here, she knows that.

When they've had enough of hanging around the neighbourhood, they go to a disco on Crémazie Boulevard. Together, they look defiantly at the bouncer, the waiters, sometimes even at other customers. They take the Métro in groups to go down to the Vieux-Port for in-line skating. In a group, they're noisy and exceptional. They pass though the various steps at top speed.

Hélène knows that.

But outside the limits of the neighbourhood, danger is lying in wait for her, not for the others. If she gets lost and ends up alone with herself, her desire will be to try violently to fade away and she won't be able to stop.

That's why she went back to the club to ask Martin to go to Marie-Pierre Sauvé's school with her. He refused, scowling with such lack of comprehension that Hélène immediately felt betrayed. She has understood: this time he has clearly rejected her. She turned her back on him, swearing that she'll never set foot in this dump again.

That's his tough luck, she thought.

Anyway, for the time being all that matters is the place she's going to.

She unfolds a map on her bed to look for the street where the school is. Where Marie-Pierre Sauvé went every day till the end of June, like other girls her age from her neighbourhood or maybe of her species — those already fated by nature to a violent death. The place she was supposed to go back to next September. If that man hadn't stopped her along her way. If he hadn't raped her and then strangled her. If he hadn't left her to rot who knows where before deciding to discard her on Île de la Merci, the island of the first time, the island of memories that no longer resemble real life.

Four more Métro stations. After that, she'll walk along a boulevard, cross a street, and then the school will appear. If she goes on, if she takes another few steps, she'll discover the family house where Marie-Pierre Sauvé's parents and her brother live.

Hélène knows that because everything is in the papers.

She takes one last look at her reflection in the mirror at the front door. When she was ten, to avoid seeing herself in the mirror she'd open the door of the medicine chest whenever she went into the bathroom. Now she can't even cross the threshold of the house without glancing in the mirror. Doing so disgusts her. Punishment — not to look at herself in the front-door mirror for at least one week. Her mother does it whenever she goes out. She'll rearrange a lock of hair. Her father does it — he salutes, like a character in a war movie. Now and then Lisa does it too — she murmurs something she's learned in one of her books about history, dreams, or mythology. But not her. Not her!

She works at the garage till early afternoon. Every half-hour she puts her hand in her pocket to check that the name of the school and the street are still there, waiting for her.

At one o'clock José arrives and offers to drive Hélène to the Métro. She has told him where she's going. If anyone can understand her, he can. But José isn't thinking about that story today. He's already preoccupied by another one.

In his gleaming car he tells Hélène that a father fired three times through a closet door and that his nine-year-old little girl was shot above her right breast, beneath her navel and in her hip. He adds, wiping his face on his shirt-sleeve, that the man then hanged himself. And the mother? Hélène wants to ask.

When she gets out of the car she slams the door, muttering that he has no right to tell her things like that. Especially not today.

José shrugs and drives away.

It must be because of the corpse on the island, Hélène thinks. Or because of the neighbourhood. It's not just José, everybody here is obsessed to some extent. It must be because they've all grown up or lived too close to the prison. For if she is constantly aware of its presence, everyone else must be too. They must all have feared that some day or other a prisoner would escape. Their houses are so close, so accessible to the madness of a person who has been locked up for all those months. Two years less a day, her father explained to her, that's the maximum time a prisoner can serve there. Luckily for her that's not where Marie-Pierre Sauvé's murderer will be locked up. If they ever find him, of course. If they ever lock him up.

During the trip in the Métro, Hélène tries to imagine what the ceremony will be like. She feels a kind of curiosity tinged with anger. An infinite anger. She has to become acquainted once and for all with the world as it is.

She thinks about what Martin told her the other night: "Imagine you're facing up to somebody." At the school, sitting among all the others, it's still to herself that she'll have to face up. She's going to pay tribute to that girl because she was murdered, because she, Hélène, could have been in her place.

Marie-Pierre Sauvé's school resembles hers: a red-brick front, lots of windows. In the summer, Hélène has often noticed, the layer of air that encloses certain schools is nearly identical to the one that surrounds the jail. It's the boundary between the known and the unknown, between one reality that is not experienced fully and another that's not altogether imagined. A time that cannot be the present.

Hélène stands there, not daring to step forward.

She spots a few people at the door and all at once she grasps the scale of what is happening. The event swells inside her like an article of clothing in a gust of wind.

I have to go there, she tells herself.

So she follows a group of girls who are holding each other's hands and goes inside the school.

Her girlfriends. All her girlfriends. There's a false serenity on their faces and in each of their movements. Hélène watches them; they're smiling, like Marie-Pierre Sauvé in her photo. They're dressed cheerfully. After all, it's a tribute, almost a kind of celebration.

But it's so dark, thinks Hélène. So profoundly dark.

Clothes must contain an essence of what the wearer is thinking, that's what Hélène has always believed. And so her mother's white gown in the wedding photo was insane. Her own clothes at this very moment, the colours here, the smiles: insane.

The gymnasium has been fixed up for the event. The graffiti on the walls of the corridor have been erased; it's done every summer. No sign of violence. No vulgarity.

The ashes have been placed on a table covered with a white cloth. There are masses of flowers around the urn. And behind it, on the wall, again the photo of Marie-Pierre Sauvé. Always the same one. As if there have never been any others. As if people wanted to be sure that everyone recognizes the person to whom they've come to pay tribute. The one who is resting in the urn. She is here. With us. It's where she is sleeping and it's all right to smile, she would have wanted to see you smile because now she is sleeping in peace.

This is the first time Hélène has seen an urn and now she can form a clear picture of how little remains of a human body. She is sitting on a straight-backed chair, slightly off to the side. She can't slip inside the event. The atmosphere inside the school is even more unstable than outside. What one is supposed to think or feel isn't written down anywhere, not on any wall or any face.

The group of girls has taken seats at the front with the other pupils in the class and they're still holding each other's hands.

The principal arrives a little later, followed by the parents. They too are holding hands. Hélène looks at them, certain they're going to collapse, but the damage has already been done and marks every one of their pores. They're living with it. They're breathing. Everyone here is breathing.

Does she really have to believe that all this is life? wonders Hélène.

And now one of the girls in the group gets up and starts to recite a poem.

She passes over the horror.

Then it's the turn of the mother, the brother, other friends to talk.

And memories of the dead girl start to fly around everywhere in the gym.

All at once everything becomes familiar, except for Hélène.

Except for the reporter leaning against the back wall.

Except for the boy Hélène spots on his way in, head high, body stiff and sombre as a crow's.

A single knot of emotions is tangible. But the rest, all the rest seems so unreal.

This isn't true, says the boy's gaze to Hélène.

Not possible, says Hélène's gaze.

If there is a bridge that leads to the understanding of such an event, neither of them has seen it, neither of them wants to cross it.

Just as the principal began to talk, Hélène felt a disordered heat travelling down through her body, and she got up to rush to the bathroom. In any event, she couldn't listen to any more. One more word and she'd start to yell.

The tribute has been paid and now all those present are clinging to one another, are rooted there, not daring to leave the gym. Those people are alive and Marie-Pierre Sauvé is not. Never again will she be alive. As soon as they've walked through the door of the school, they'll have proof of it. The proof will be provided by the normal passing of the rest of the day.

Hélène hasn't found out anything. Throughout the ceremony she was on guard, on the outside, when what she wanted to do was go inside so she could understand the rule. Something else has to happen, but she doesn't know what.

She sees Martin again, training so he can control everything. His feet and his hands in action. The trainer told him to be a moving target. That's it exactly. Those words are for her. She is the moving target.

Standing in front of the big mirror in the bathroom, she thinks about the number of times that Marie-Pierre Sauvé must have come here to look at herself. Several times a day she must have brushed her long hair over the sink. She would open a big purse, rummage through the contents, then take out a round brush for curly hair, accidentally dropping some change. She'd have shot an amused look at one of her friends.

Marie-Pierre Sauvé's movements materialize easily before Hélène's eyes. She can almost feel the girl's presence. Above all, she'd like to have a quick glance at what was in her purse and

what was in her locker. To amass clues that would reveal a human life that was so fragile. So obedient to the law of others. A hairbrush, an address book, a good luck charm, some keys in a purse. A few hairs in a washbasin. Some inconsequential words exchanged in front of the mirror.

Hélène leaves the bathroom.

And that's when she spots the boy she had noticed in the gym a little earlier. He's leaning against a locker. This time, it occurs to her that he could be the boy whose photo she'd seen in the paper: maybe Marie-Pierre Sauvé's boyfriend? Maybe her murderer? She goes over to him.

Like her, he left the gym before everyone else, and now, Hélène assumes, he doesn't know where to go. Maybe he's hoping for a sign from someone. Maybe he even followed her and has been waiting for her. Maybe this is where he often waited for Marie-Pierre Sauvé.

He is leaning against the locker, shoulders slightly hunched. Even from a distance, Hélène can sense his anger. Anger that's alive, uncontrollable, full of roots. Altogether different from Martin's.

He raises his head, looks at her in turn.

It's up to her to make the next move, because she is the moving target. To approach her opponent and when least expected, to slip away. At the moment of greatest heat. Because the heat has sailed along the corridors of the school and has finally chosen her body, Hélène's. The moving target that is once again approaching a boy she doesn't know. But she has to approach him. She has to talk to somebody and somebody has to talk to her. At all costs, she has to recognize her opponent. If it isn't Martin, it will be someone else.

"Was this her locker?"

The boy turns his head away and doesn't answer.

"Was she your girlfriend?"

He still doesn't answer.

Hélène goes on: "I never saw her before."

"Before what?"

He seems a little surprised.

"Before all this business."

"So what are you doing here?"

"What about you?"

"She was in my class."

It's Hélène's turn to be silent.

They stay like that for a moment, each inside his own thoughts.
Then he smiles and goes away.

She follows him.

Outside, the sun hits them in the face, as if they were coming
out of several months of detention.

On the steps, a crowd has gathered around Marie-Pierre Sauvé's
parents. They've finally managed to leave, all together, friends,
pupils, parents, and now they're all standing on the steps, still
reluctant to go home.

Nobody knows what I know, thinks Hélène. Nobody knows
who she is. Nobody gives a damn either. She could be anyone at
all. Merely somebody who's curious, who doesn't belong here. Or
that boy's girlfriend. They don't give a damn about him either,
Hélène was quick to notice that. No one comes over to talk to
him. Not a nod. Nothing.

He was probably the loneliest boy in his class, Hélène thinks.
Like her, he didn't belong to any group.

All year in a classroom while his own body seems to belong

to someone else. Even his desk flies through another dimension. His head, like hers, is filled with forbidden objects.

And here he is coming down the stairs, and no one is looking at him. But she keeps following him. He turns around to make sure. They're both on the sidelines, a silent islet next to such a tightly knit family.

Some things are due me, thinks Hélène. Certain things have to happen. She has manufactured her own obsession and now she knows what she knows. The number of murders. The hands, bound or not. The island, the undergrowth, the rivers. The walks through the city's deserted parks. The heat. The fists. The silence. She knows what she knows. Even if it's not much. Even if she, like that boy most likely, is outside everything.

Six

THOMAS'S ROOM

"Lisa, come down off your cloud!" Viviane exclaims.

Another Saturday. A Saturday so hot and humid that Lisa is dreaming about a great gust that could suddenly rise up above the river, pass through the trees and carry her away — only her — towards a cooler and more appealing day. For a good half-hour she's been winding a long lock of hair around her finger. It looks now like a genuine ringlet.

"That's a very bad habit," adds Viviane.

"I know," replies Lisa.

She stops for a moment, then starts again, with another lock.

But what difference does it make to her if Lisa's hair is all in ringlets? wonders Hélène.

What difference does it make if Lisa runs away to the clouds and doesn't talk?

Last night the two of them finally had a talk. Hélène heard them. Viviane started: "Lisa doesn't seem to be herself these days."

"It certainly isn't my fault," Robert replied.

And wham! End of conversation. Every word spoken here is like an accusation. A provocation. It's better to be silent. That way nothing can go any further.

Looking at Lisa, Hélène thinks that things can't be all that bad in the clouds after all.

"Samuel cried out last night," she tells her.

"He did?"

"He shouted: 'He killed my cat!'"

Lisa turns towards Samuel.

"What cat, Samuel?"

"A cat."

"I see!"

She smiles.

"And who killed it?"

"What do you think? A monster!"

"That's right, I forgot."

All those monsters lurking around Samuel! Now that she spends most of her days with him, Lisa should keep them in mind. When she and Hélène were little, a multitude of individuals lived among the furniture and objects in their room. All those voices were constantly chattering around them. The two girls were part of them. They belonged to a world filled with echoes, alongside the deaf and vast world. But then one day the heart of the vast world started to beat in the body and head of Hélène and then in Lisa's. It beats, it reverberates, but it's still deaf and offers no response.

"What'll we do today?" asks Lisa.

Hélène sticks her hand in the pocket of her overalls, as if the answer to Lisa's question might be found there. She takes out a scrap of paper on which are written the name and phone number of the boy she met at Marie-Pierre Sauvé's school.

Lisa presses her: "Are you going out again?"

"I'm not sure."

"Stay!" says Samuel.

Hélène returns the paper to her pocket.

Once more, she sees Thomas across from the Métro station. She sees the people emerging and rushing to the bus stop while the two of them stand there, unable to take their leave of one another.

They assume that it's over now, she had thought while Thomas was talking to her. Because the papers say practically nothing now about the murder of Marie-Pierre Sauvé, people have begun to think that the story is over. But a murder like that spreads. It reproduces itself. And it's always the same murder. Hélène just has to think about the facts already jotted in her notebook to be aware of that. That's the way it is. In any case, for her, for Thomas maybe, for a dozen people the murder of Marie-Pierre Sauvé will never stop happening.

Thomas.

If he's come into Hélène's life so abruptly, it was to take Martin's place. So Hélène would like to believe. Martin isn't ready for her. That's what she thinks. Thomas has big black eyes and he caught on right away to what it was that she wanted. He caught hold of a sign in the absence of a sign.

"I don't want to talk about her any more," he said.

Then he scribbled his name and phone number on a scrap of paper before rushing into the Métro.

And now?

Now, Thomas can wait: Hélène has to look after her brother and her sister.

"Ready for another comedy, Samuel?"

He's ready. He's been ready for weeks.

Lisa, too, is ready.

The three of them get up and file into the living room to see their father.

"What's daddy doing?" asks Samuel.

"He's thinking," reply Lisa and Hélène together.

Robert barely lifts his head to look at them. He doesn't smile. He chases an invisible presence from the air to signal to them to leave. The presence has nothing to do with them but since they've come into his field of vision, which is already too restricted, he chases them away like someone chasing flies.

Samuel imitates him with a frown.

Then they go outside and sit on the front steps.

Lisa starts delicately peeling little chips of white paint off the steps. She piles them up. Hélène watches her, annoyed.

"Get off my back!" Lisa demands.

Behind them, the house is barely breathing. A breath of wind through the curtains. A flow of blood in the veins.

"Who's this Thomas?" asks Lisa.

"He isn't Martin!" exclaims Samuel.

Hélène doesn't have time to reply before Lisa goes on, rather triumphantly: "She won't let you go out tonight."

"Why not?"

"Because of the murder."

Hélène's amazement. She who thought that Lisa was outside all that.

"Shut up!" she orders.

Then: "I don't intend to ask permission either."

"You'd better," replies Lisa. "And you'd better be scared, too."

She has succeeded in removing a big chip of paint without breaking it and she goes up to her room to add it to her collection.

When she comes back down, Hélène and Samuel are on the boulevard. She runs to catch up with them.

"Where are we going?"

"The jail."

Samuel opens his eyes wide, clutching Hélène's hand very tightly.

The Bordeaux jail is just far enough away that, for him, merely getting there is an adventure. They have to cross the railway tracks and walk along the big Parc de la Visitation before they arrive at the strange building. All three of them on Gouin Boulevard, in the sunlight, for just a few minutes. For Samuel, an eternity.

And then they pace the wall in front of the jail, inventing as they do whenever they go there stories of revenge, of punishment, with handcuffs, bars — the whole arsenal, shrouded in mystery and fear, especially in Samuel's eyes. From the street, it's impossible to see the prisoners when they go out into the inner courtyard. None of the three has yet seen a paddy wagon. But they can easily picture the prisoners scrambling out of it, then spitting before they go in the front door, across from the Notre-Dame-de-la-Merci hospital, that other jail one never leaves; a

place to die: a phrase they don't say but that is part of the words long since whispered by the walls of the house, by the street, the park, the river.

The hospital may have been located there precisely to remove any urge to die, Hélène often says, and to show that there are worse things. Because the prisoners are going to be locked up for days and days, it could scare them to death before they've even started to serve their sentences. Or not at all, she sometimes thinks. They don't give a damn because it's no better outside. That's why they spit. There's a sort of corruption in the air which means that it could quite possibly make no difference to them, for a moment, to go inside.

"What did they do?" asks Samuel.

"Some of them stole money from a store," replies Lisa.

"They bashed somebody's head against a wall," adds Hélène, "non-stop. They broke into a house and beat up the person who was asleep on the sofa."

"Is it really in the shape of a star?" asks Samuel again.

And again: "Can they watch TV?"

The thought of it delights him: each in his own little cell with his own little TV set!

"When the death penalty still existed," says Lisa suddenly, "it was there, in the dome, that the prisoners were hanged."

"It was not," says Hélène. "They did it outside."

"Are you sure? What about that story about the prisoner who was hanged in the dome?"

"It may be just a legend."

"Legends are always true," says Lisa.

"Anyway, the door never opens when we're there. We'd have to know when visiting hours are."

"Visitors!" exclaims Samuel.

He squeezes Hélène's hand even tighter: if that door should open! If all three of them were pushed inside by a violent wind or through some error!

He takes Lisa's hand too.

No danger, they're here! a voice inside Samuel whispers.

And so the walk to the jail invariably takes him to the heart of that power: being with them.

I'm with them, Samuel reminds himself. With them.

Hélène and Lisa would like to free their hands, they'd like the game to be over, but it's the same every time, the jail ends up frightening Samuel, it's what he wants, and the three of them stand there, shackled more by their imaginations than by anything else.

Back at the house, Samuel draws walls, a dome, high, barred windows, branching underground passages. He is preparing for his own escape.

⚜

It's the law of the family, murmurs Hélène. To defend oneself. In all circumstances.

She drops her bag onto a bench across from the Métro and sits down to wait for Thomas.

Lisa was wrong: Viviane let her go out. Shrugged: "I'm not responsible for what happens to you any more." Which means, to Hélène: "You're leaving me alone so I'm not responsible for anything."

The law of the family: a circle in the middle of the world, a jail in the shape of a star.

"Girls your age have boyfriends," said Robert to Hélène.

And, indirectly, to Lisa.

Again this business about boyfriends! Again that irreproachable need to drive the children outside. Each has his role to play: another law of families. But the circles get bigger near the borders. Harder and harder to control.

Hélène is there now. At the border.

And now Thomas is making his way towards her, suspicious, ready to take off at the first false step by Hélène, at the slightest look revealing a distance between them that can't be crossed.

He advances, twisting the hem of his sweater with the fingers of his left hand.

Thomas and the others: a connection at once necessary and so inadequate.

Hélène looks at him, a little surprised. She hadn't noticed how handsome he was. So tall. Such dark eyes. She hadn't thought about him that way: he's handsome. His mother must have told him so a thousand times. His aunts. His girlfriends. Some of his teachers, too. But her? She has never thought about anyone in those terms, any more than her own mother has; she has never considered the existence of human beauty. Especially not in a boy her age.

She looks down at the ground; it's her turn now to stiffen on her bench. She'll never get used to it, even if it's what she wants. She'll never be able to accept the fact that he's handsome, that he's there, and that he touches her. Nor will she be able to accept it if he doesn't. She won't be able to accept the fact that she wants to. A clear, straightforward, normal desire.

He doesn't touch her. He stands there facing her and asks her what she wants to do. No hello, no introductory remarks.

"Whatever," replies Hélène.

It's still early, seven o'clock, and there's this whole evening to spend. A whole evening to be careful about what she does, to compose her face, to select her words. It isn't natural, she concludes. With Martin, something was natural; with him, nothing will ever be. Yet she gets up, ready to follow him wherever he wants.

"Think!" Hélène orders the part of herself that she hates.

Someone is there, but it's as if there were no one. There is Thomas, but his eyes never light on her. He looks around everywhere at once. They walk together towards his house, but it's as if only she were there.

They go around a park, past the school.

The farther they go, the more Hélène's body encroaches on the space. The more present and weightier it becomes. And the more transparent Thomas's body becomes.

It was her idea to go to his place. A mistake. She doesn't know why she said it, but she did. Anywhere but here. Not my place. Not the island. Your place?

They walk along the street together. She doesn't know him. She knows that his mother works nights. That his father has gone for good. So they'll soon be in an empty house where her body will become more and more invasive. It will become gigantic! If only she could shrink. Or sit very upright on a chair. If she could manage to control at least part of the space that she occupies.

"Here we are," says Thomas.

Here.

She walks inside. Quickly tries to find her place in the living room.

They get something to drink.

Thomas stands up and sits down again. He talks. He shows things to Hélène. Magazines. Photographs. He leaves the room for a moment, then comes back.

"I hate this house," he says.

He beckons to Hélène to follow him.

They go to the kitchen to get more beer.

They haven't exchanged more than fifty or so remarks since they first met at the school, and here they are, trapped in Thomas's room.

With Martin, Hélène repeats to herself, things would happen differently. Things would happen, period.

Thomas chooses a record and Hélène lets herself be carried away by the music. The beer has started to soften her thoughts.

She sniffs.

"I must be allergic to the carpet," she says.

Thomas's room is the very opposite of hers. A wall covered with graffiti, a black carpet, red curtains, appalling disorder.

Hélène laughs nervously and bites her lips. Thomas has dirty fingernails. It's surprising for someone so transparent.

It's nearly nine already. The minutes whirl around her while Thomas talks about himself, and then about them. "I don't know what I am," most of his remarks seem to say.

Hélène listens to him for a moment, then she gets up from her chair and sits next to him on the bed.

"Did she ever come here?"

"Who?"

"Marie-Pierre Sauvé."

The boy's jaws go tense.

"Did you come here just to talk about her?"

"Never mind."

She scrutinizes the walls of the room again, then she moves closer to him, she shuts her eyes, two, three, four seconds and that's it, something in her collapses, it's like an eddy, like quicksand, or a haste, yes, a kind of haste for no apparent reason. She takes a big gulp of beer to calm the powerful waters of the river that's stirring inside her body. If she goes on, she'll be carried away. She swigs more beer.

It's just me, it's just Thomas who has just put his hand on my hair.

It's just two people in a bedroom, not the entire earth that is turning, not the entire world full of a lack of understanding, not the murder, or the jail, or her brother, or her sister. She shuts her eyes, she opens her eyes. When it spins, declared one of her girlfriends, hang on to the curtains. Focus on an object, she'd said, laughing with her mouth wide open.

Hélène would like to lie down with Thomas and snuggle up to him: impossible, something's escaping her.

Now he's kissing her. No more awkward than any other transparent being, she thinks. No heavier than any other boy his age. Her own body, gigantic and limp, is caught in a whirlwind.

Thomas's tongue is small and hard, luckily. Hélène lets him do as he wants. She ought to react, to respond to what Thomas is doing. But she doesn't. The walls of the room are closing in on her. So it goes.

Thomas has taken off his sweater. Slowly he pulls off Hélène's. She doesn't want to. She doesn't want him to look at her. Or touch her.

But Thomas's skin is so soft. And the walls of the room are so close now.

He presses on her shoulders so she'll lie down, then he stretches out beside her.

It's not the first time. He knows what he's doing.

He half-rises, bends over Hélène and unzips her jeans. Slips his hand inside as best he can.

Hélène stiffens. Why that? Why right away? She grits her teeth. It's hard and harsh. He goes on. She bites his shoulder.

Thomas doesn't understand.

"Stop," says Hélène.

Now she pushes him.

"Not here," she says.

"What do you mean, not here?"

"Not here, that's all."

Thomas stands up and kicks the wall.

"I drank too much," she adds.

But she thinks the opposite; she hasn't drunk enough. Definitely not. She gropes around for her sweater and pulls it on hastily.

"Okay," says Thomas.

He tries to control himself.

"Okay, not here."

He sits down beside her again, his head in his hands.

"Stay a while," he asks.

"No."

"Why not?"

"My mother'll kill me."

Suddenly Hélène panics.

"I have to go, fast."

She gets up, leaves the room, tries to find the bathroom.

A door, slam. Another.

"Where's the bathroom?" she sobs.

There has to be a bathroom. Slam. This door has to be it.

Eventually she finds it. She turns on the light and sits on the edge of the tub to get her breath back.

"I'll never be able to," she murmurs.

She gets up, washes her hands, splashes cold water on her face, then disappears into the hallway, onto the stairs, into the street.

Thomas comes after her.

"You can't just go like that," he shouts.

He catches up with her and tries to hold her in his arms. But it's ridiculous to hold such a big girl in his arms and Hélène frees herself fairly quickly.

"What did I do?" asks Thomas.

"It's not you, it's me," says Hélène. "It's my fault. It's me."

"But what is it?"

"I'm not normal."

Thomas can't help laughing.

"Me neither!"

"For me though, it's true," says Hélène, "it's true."

Then there appear before her: the jail, the notebook, and her body, booby-trapped like a minefield.

Afterwards, in her room, when she wasn't expecting it, Hélène senses Thomas's presence. More clearly, more intensely than when he was with her.

The idea of Thomas is more powerful than Thomas.

She knows it.

In the middle of the night she wakes up in the room with the black carpet. She recognizes the smell. The disorder.

Something has to stop. She opens the window and throws herself into the void.

⚜

Lisa is standing beside her bed and asking her how it was.

"Let me sleep."

"You're finished sleeping," Lisa goes on, lifting the sheet.

Hélène moans. She still feels so tired.

"Why'd you do that?"

"Tell me how it was!"

"Get the hell out of here!" says Hélène.

The day is getting off to a bad start. Why does Lisa get up so early? Hélène always feels as if she hasn't slept enough. She'd like to go back to the dream in which she jumps out the window. She'd like to go back to Thomas's room and start over. Feel his weight on her again. Any weight at all except the one that has her nailed down here.

It's barely seven o'clock and Viviane is already in the kitchen making coffee. Hélène hears her slippers shuffling across the floor. That sound sometimes drives her crazy.

Soon her father will come out of the bedroom too, that's why her mother is hurrying. To have a few minutes of peace before she's forced to talk.

Viviane is working this afternoon. She'll apply her makeup,

put on her red dress, give Hélène advice and leave. Another charming couple will come to visit the house on Tanguay Street: she'll have to convince them that happiness exists. Wasn't she herself blindly convinced of that several years ago when she bought the white house? Why shouldn't they be too? Why not perpetuate the lie?

Hélène has brought the newspaper up to her room. She knows the police are still looking for witnesses. Is she a witness?

She leafs through the paper eagerly as if she were looking for her own photo.

No suspect has been apprehended so far and it won't be happening for a while, Hélène is sure. Some of the murders marked down in her notebook are over two years old and no murderer has been arrested yet.

She thinks back to the route she took to get to Thomas's place. Marie-Pierre Sauvé would have taken nearly the same route home. No one knows yet why the murderer brought the body to the island. Marie-Pierre Sauvé was on her way to a friend's place, east of the Bordeaux neighbourhood; could he have been following her since she left her house? Or maybe he'd been hanging around near the Métro station and that was where he had noticed her. He would have taken her by force to his place, not far from Saint-Réal Street. Why not? And a few days later he brought the body to the island because he had to put it somewhere. He too had most likely played on the island when he was a child and later on, he'd come there like all the others, with his first girlfriend. Which was why he'd chosen that spot, Hélène thinks. He laid down the body and folded the clothing.

He must still be prowling around nearby. Maybe he's followed her too. Maybe he comes to the garage for gas. Impossible to forget.

Samuel has stuck his head in the doorway.

"What're you doing?"

"I'm busy."

He holds out his owl book.

"Please, Lène."

"Not today, Samuel."

But Samuel acts as if he hasn't heard, he stands there waiting for her to make up her mind.

"Okay," says Hélène, rolling her eyes. "Come and sit down. But this is the last time, promise?"

"Promise."

He sits close to her and Hélène finally opens the book.

"Owls live in the forest," she begins. "When they come into town they massacre the pigeons!"

"They massacre pigeons?"

Samuel is flabbergasted. He looks at his sister, mouth wide open.

Hélène wishes she could bang her head against the wall.

Why did I say that? Why?

Samuel starts to yell: "They do not! It doesn't say that in the book!"

"I know, Samuel, I know. That was a joke."

A tiny little joke.

But he's too furious to understand; he yanks the book out of Hélène's hands and throws it onto the floor.

"You're mean!"

He can't stop. He picks up the book and starts ripping out the pages.

"Don't do that!" Hélène shouts in turn.

She grabs him by the arm so he can't do it. A moment later he stops, looks at his book and bursts out sobbing.

"It's my fault," says Hélène in a feeble voice.

It's my fault.

Samuel seems to have forgotten it all too quickly.

Viviane comes home empty-handed from her meeting with the charming couple.

"Yesterday we went to the jail," Samuel tells her.

"I told you not to take him there!" she explodes.

"What difference does it make?" replies Hélène.

"It's not a place for a five-year-old or for Lisa!"

"And what about here?"

Pointless rejoinder. Yet another vain provocation. Hélène knows it. So does Viviane, but she has to force herself not to reply. She goes up to her room to change.

"You did that on purpose," Hélène tells Samuel.

A little later, she explains to him about the things they have to keep secret.

"Going to the jail is a secret that mummy mustn't know about. That she can't understand."

"What else?"

"Going to see Martin train."

"What else?"

"Lots of other things, you'll see."

Samuel thinks it over.

Then he says: "Lisa's got more secrets."

"That's true," says Hélène. "She's really weird."

"True," says Samuel.

And now Hélène is totally forgiven.

⚓

In fact, no one knows where Lisa is.

The wind changes direction so quickly in the house that they've lost Lisa without realizing it. Lisa's presence is so slight that no one even knows how long it has been since she's been there.

"A new secret," declares Samuel.

Robert isn't listening. He has already driven all over the neighbourhood and just now he's wondering if he ought to be getting really upset.

"Lisa would never do that."

"What do you mean, never?" asks Hélène.

She's not too sure what he means by that. Lisa isn't her, she'd never do that. It's true that Lisa never leaves the house without saying goodbye. She says good morning when she gets up, goodbye when she leaves, hello when she comes back. Lisa asks permission. Lisa would never do that. Run away, that must be what he meant. It would be perfectly normal if Hélène did that. But Lisa. That's not the way her father thinks of her. Surely he'd prefer it to be Hélène. Maybe he even hopes she'll do it so that the threat will finally stop staring them in the face. But Lisa?

"All right, no need to get all worked up," he concludes.

Viviane looks at him, flustered.

Hélène, sitting at the table with them, furtively watches her mother. She has a good idea what's going through her mind.

Don't think about the murderer who's on the loose, she pleads silently.

Her mother has asked her several times to talk to Lisa, try to find out why she's upset. Hélène hasn't done so and now Lisa isn't here, and once again it's her fault.

Only Samuel seems not very worried. He even seems to be enjoying himself. For once they aren't squabbling. He comes to sit at the table and asks for his supper.

Hélène gets up to serve him. If we carry on as if nothing's wrong, she thinks, Lisa will come back. In any case, Lisa isn't her: she will come back.

Lisa isn't me.

Without a word, Hélène serves everyone and they tuck into their meal. A kind of peace descends, like when a storm that has been forecast finally arrives.

Robert and Viviane look at Lisa with the same discouraging thought: not another one, no, not her too.

"Where have you been?" Robert asks her.

"I went to the park for a walk."

Lisa, usually so obedient, hadn't seen the time pass.

"But I looked all over for you!"

"Why didn't you say you were going out?" asks Viviane. "With everything that's going on now!"

"And what park?" Robert insists. "I looked all over."

Lisa looks down. Her cheeks turn red: a flame has just burst inside her.

"Leave me alone."

"Fine. Leave her alone," says Viviane.

Hélène can't believe her ears: leave her alone! And what about her, why won't they ever leave *her* alone?

She follows Lisa upstairs.

"I'll tell you what happened with Thomas if you'll tell me where you really went."

"Just to the park!"

"Yes, but what happened?"

"Nothing. Absolutely nothing. What amazing thing could happen to me anyway?"

"What do you mean? It seems to me the slightest thing could be amazing to you!"

"That's true. Life is so amazing!"

The sun has just gone from Lisa's room. She lies down on her bed to savour its presence a little longer. Shuts her eyes.

She could well be lying for once.

She could say that she sat with the group of boys and girls who hang out at the chalet in the park and that she found out some horrifying things about the murder. She knows she could shut Hélène up with that story. She could say that the police questioned them one after another, which would be only a half-lie because the police are always patrolling the area, especially around the parks.

"I wrote a letter to Florence," she finally confesses.

She takes the rough draft from her pocket.

"You did?" says Hélène. "I heard you talking to her on the phone last night. Do you still want to go and visit her?"

"Not really."

"But you talked about it so much!"

Lisa gets off her bed. She stows the draft in her desk.

"What about you?"

"Me?"

Hélène tries to think of the best way to sum up the situation. She knows very well what Lisa wants to hear.

"I tried, but I couldn't do it."

"I'll never be able to either."

They start to snicker.

"It was nice at first," says Hélène. "Then there was a moment that was harder . . ."

"When was that?"

"I don't know how to say it."

Their thoughts take off then in every direction, which happens every time they bring up this subject.

They're at the park, in a bedroom, in Thomas's bed. They are trying to understand the moment that's as hard as a rock. They see again images from movies where everything is a lie, according to Hélène. Especially people's features. The sighs of ecstasy. Hélène is absolutely convinced of the existence of that lie on a global scale. And so they have to sink into something darker and more unsettling. The constant back-and-forth movement around them, reproduction, copulation, communion; the laws of nature reminding them that it exists, that it's the very essence of life. In the darkness of forests. In the mud, on the banks of rivers. In the yard, under their window. The yowling of cats. The dogs they saw once when they were little, right beside them, the big one crushing the little one with his full weight. The unbearably human movements of monkeys on branches. They bury themselves beneath the earth where there are those thousands of little rodents. Then, following the example of animals, those billions of humans in billions of houses, cars, back lanes, parks.

"It's disgusting," says Lisa.

They burst out laughing again.

"Most of the girls in my class liked it," adds Hélène.

So it shouldn't be so terrible for us!

She feels Thomas's warm body.

She feels her own skin as if it were someone else's: suddenly full of promises and density.

Lisa's body on the contrary has already disappeared.

Seven

THE ORDEAL

*H*ow to bear this burden?

The friends of Marie-Pierre Sauvé laid flowers on the island in the spot where her body had been found.

At the garage, José greets Hélène with that news. He rolls up his sleeves as if he has some crucial task to perform. He sniffs his ink-stained fingers. He thinks he has grasped the depths of the human soul. But he chews his gum with a look on his face like that of a lost animal.

Hélène would like to place a little of her pain on the island, too.

Her parents are unhappy and, already, she bears that burden, too. Slowly, very slowly it has become encrusted in her pores. To it has now been added the responsibility for Samuel's happiness. And now Lisa's. And Thomas's.

ise Turcotte

I don't love him, she thinks every time as she hangs up the phone.

Which doesn't stop her from calling him ten times a day, or sucking to the marrow his slightest attempt to resist.

Thomas's mother brings home dishes prepared by the caterer she works for. He sits in the green kitchen over quail with grapes, veal Marengo, coquilles Saint-Jacques. Sometimes she eats with him. Sometimes not. Always, he thinks about Hélène.

He goes out with his friends two or three nights in a row. He drinks a lot of beer. That doesn't stop him from painting walls for the neighbours. Several are repainting their houses this summer. They believe in fresh starts. He only thinks about Hélène.

At fifteen, when you think about someone that way it's as if you've been lifted off the ground and then released all at once. The thought of the other is a weight that drags us towards the depths.

I don't like him, thinks Hélène. She opens her eyes and Thomas's face slips away at once. Only a sense of unease remains suspended in the still-hot August air.

She didn't want a boy her own age. She followed Thomas because of Marie-Pierre Sauvé. Now she could nearly touch the words he doesn't say and his dreams of vertigo.

Her father would say, with a smile: *that's life*. Things want us before we want them. They desire us, we say yes, and that's that.

The wedding photo expands before Hélène as if it were on a giant screen. Not a hint of concern in their smiles. Not a hint of doubt. Marriage wanted them. So what happened after that?

Hélène has heard it said that children are born because they want to be. She believes that's a lie. They're born and undesired

104

parents go on taking root in the house.

Hélène certainly won't have children and it's no one's fault in particular.

She'll bring Thomas to her house. Show him the island, even if he doesn't want to see it. After all, you have to surmount certain facts of existence. If she is still obsessed by the murder and by a past from which she is excluded, he'll have to accept it. After that he can do what he wants to her.

For the first time, she thinks about the money she'll earn over the summer. She could throw it out her bedroom window. She could squander it in one night with Thomas. She could do whatever she wanted.

A sensation of furtive and suspect power goes through her.

There has to be a change.

She has to change.

It has to affect her face, her hair, her arms, her clothes. Even the past, even the others around her.

⚜

In Hélène's absence, Lisa is looking after Samuel. She keeps chewing at the ends of her braids. She sometimes spends hours at a time sitting in the yard, motionless, this time training herself to disappear into a genuine limbo. But her power is limited.

"How does a person imagine nothing?" she asks Samuel.

"Nothing is all black," he replies, after closing his eyes.

"No," she tells him. "It's white."

Computers aren't selling. Neither are houses. Robert and Viviane come home more tired than ever. They have that in common.

"There's nothing worse than feeling useless," Robert always says.

Nothing worse then being bored to death, Viviane could add. But she says nothing.

She still sees herself as a young girl dying of boredom at home. But that, she can't tell him. If she looks back she has to admit that it's always been like that. She's bored, but hasn't the slightest idea of exactly what that means. When the girls were little, she did what had to be done, with a smile, she played with each of them in the light of the living room, but always there was that empty space, that nothingness which attracted the greater part of her. At the park, at the mall, with women friends, her body is as present as an empty shell on the beach. She can't even imagine what it is that she might desire. She can think about an African safari because she's seen one in a movie, or about a hotel room to rest in because it is something she's done. And that's more or less it. Most of all, she never pictures herself in the company of others who are close to her.

The house isn't big enough, this is the easy conclusion she's come to. It's why she is sitting at the kitchen table, over plans drawn by an apprentice architect. After she has enlarged the kitchen, renovated the bathroom, redecorated the living room, all that was left was to fix up a room in the attic. The house doesn't have a basement.

"It's a room for me," she informs Robert by means of a thousand hints.

In any case, he couldn't care less. This time he really doesn't give a shit.

Still imbued with her new will, Hélène decides to walk past the club in case Martin is there. What she'd like of course is to walk by him with Thomas. She sees him leaving the club in a rage, coming up to her and shaking her. She'd like to cast a little shadow on his life. She'd like him to scare her and after that, fall to his knees. She knows that he could. That thought brushes against her; she must dispel it.

She walks past the club without even looking.

Because this she also knows: even if Martin were there, even if he noticed her, he wouldn't come out.

She turns at the traffic lights and arrives at the house.

From the gallery, if she stands on tiptoe she can see the river. As for the island, she can only sense its presence: a great body always hidden in the darkness. A familiar body. Foreign. Which one only thinks about.

Hélène smiles.

Tonight Thomas will come and maybe — but it's a slim possibility — maybe she'll no longer be the only one who senses that presence.

Think about the island, she'll tell him.

Look at the river.

She's so lucky, everyone says, to live so close to a river. One that runs peacefully behind the house. A river full of fish. Full of mud. Of tadpoles. Polluted. Running peacefully day after day behind the house.

"I don't believe it!" she exclaims when she notices the plans on the table. Her good mood has just crashed to the floor.

She wants to pick up the plans and study them more closely, but Viviane stops her abruptly.

"Wash your hands first. There's grease all over them."

Hélène looks at her hands, then at her mother.

"It's in your head," she hisses.

She washed them twice before she left the garage, she always does, but now she washes them again. She insists on seeing the plans. She insists on knowing at once what they've cooked up this time.

"It won't be like when we did the kitchen," says Viviane. "It's upstairs, you won't even know it's going on."

Oh sure, this time they'll be pounding on her head. Hélène can't bear it when work is done in the house. Nothing must move here. Everything has its place and it must stay there. And then the dust, the noise, the impatient shouts. Her parents always on the verge of a nervous breakdown, because the end of the work must at all costs mark the end of their failure. Finally, worst of all, is the resumption of normal life, as if nothing has changed. Nothing has changed, Viviane's grey eyes always end up saying. Nothing will ever change.

"It's pointless," declares Hélène, replacing the plans on the table.

Viviane gives her a contemptuous look.

"Enthusiastic as ever!"

She gets herself something to drink and a moment later, Hélène mounts a fresh attack.

"I invited somebody for supper."

"What do you mean? Who?"

"Thomas. A guy."

Viviane is surprised. Hélène has never had many male friends. Nor has Lisa, for that matter. And suddenly, there's this Thomas. And she, the mother, didn't even know that he existed. Maybe her daughter is like other girls after all.

"That's fine," she says.

She does her best to smile, not daring to ask any questions for fear that Hélène might change her mind.

Thomas didn't even have time to cross the threshold before Samuel threw himself at his legs. A kind of battle got under way and Hélène had to wait till the end of hostilities before she could get close to Thomas.

"That's his way of welcoming you," she told him, pulling him by the arm.

Lisa came downstairs almost immediately. Then Viviane and Robert materialized, shaking hands with Thomas in an absolutely official way.

Samuel continued to dog his footsteps.

Hélène told him several times to leave Thomas alone, wondering how they were all coming across. A starving family who've never seen another soul!

Now she tries to overcome the embarrassment that is slowly taking hold of her.

They're all sitting around the table in the garden.

They pounce on Thomas.

Each in turn asks questions, it doesn't matter what, as long as they're saying something, as long as Thomas replies, as long as something gets said.

Hélène is silent.

She's a member of this family of starving wolves.

She prays for the meal to be over. For the pack to disperse!

Actually, Thomas feels quite comfortable here in this garden where everything grows rather freely. The hedges haven't been clipped yet. The flowers are faded.

Robert follows Thomas's gaze and apologizes: the weather, the unusually hot summer. This launches him into a long chain of explanations, trying awkwardly to win Thomas's complicity.

But Thomas couldn't care less: at this very moment he's thinking about the pasta with seafood that's still waiting for him at home, and the thought makes him want to laugh.

He also wants very much to kiss Hélène.

Suddenly she seems younger to him, more remote, more . . . he doesn't know what, really. He could swear that she's behaving as if he weren't there.

He answers Robert's questions, concealing entire segments of truth. He guesses what he can't say, for instance where he and Hélène met. Hélène watches him out of the corner of her eye. He doesn't feel like talking about his own father either, or about school or about dishes with seafood — and even less about his mother.

Impassive, Hélène listens to him lie. It makes no difference to her. Her parents seem delighted, especially Robert, he can't stop talking, he tries to sell every one of his pitiful ideas to Thomas. It's another diversion. She hears the cry on the island and she wants to stand up, to leave behind the genuine lie which isn't in Thomas's mouth.

The lie doesn't come from Thomas's mouth, she wants to shout. To shout. She grips Thomas's wrist hard enough to startle him.

"Come on, we're going for a walk."

One final piece of advice from Robert and they're alone on the boulevard, as Hélène has been hoping.

Now she's angry at having seen Thomas behave, despite his lies, like a member of the family. A member of society, a member of the world, when she wants him to be outside with her.

I'll show him, she thinks, as if she were going to announce a punishment.

Chastisement, punishment: these words will always affect her and resonate in her in one way or another.

They arrive at the island.

She takes Thomas's hand and tells him: "Here it is."

Thomas focuses his gaze as far away as possible. He would like to leave here but he can't. His classmate's face appears to him clearly for the first time since her death, and he stands there motionless. He has to go there. He's so close to the spot that's been talked about so much around him, at school and in the papers, that he can't step away from it now.

"I just want to see if there really are flowers."

"Okay," says Thomas. "It's like a visit to the graveyard."

"That's right, a visit to the graveyard."

There are flowers.

Hélène and Thomas inspect them in silence. They find nothing to say to one another.

The flowers are tied together in wreaths, lying along the shore past where Marie-Pierre Sauvé's body was found.

Hélène would like to show Thomas the position of the body and the exact place where it was left, but she's frightened by such precision.

There must be another wreath because there are petals floating on the river.

Actually, all these flowers make her think about a wedding. A story that may have started well but ended badly. Someone could have left the party, then flung the flowers as if they were insults, and suddenly the future would have shrunk, shrunk until it no longer existed.

In a sense, it amounts to the same thing: something has ended badly, the ground has slipped beneath someone's feet.

But it's light now and it takes an effort to imagine, here in this place, a young girl's murdered body.

If it were dark, Hélène could picture once again the whiteness of the corpse. She could go back and for the nth time, imagine the worst.

Thomas has already started to visualize the face in the mud, part of the hair soaking in this dirty water.

He's so close to Hélène now. He's afraid of being too close.

He hadn't thought about it a lot before, not in these terms anyway, about the corpse, the blood, the horror; that is, he'd thought about the death of a friend from his class, about the injustice of that death, he'd thought about the rape too, about that brute of the same sex as him who rapes and kills, and it was that in particular that had angered him. A somewhat abstract anger. A generalized hatred. But here in this graveyard it's the face of Marie-Pierre he sees again, an actual face that the end of the world has just struck with the blows of an axe.

If only Hélène would stop talking.

But she questions him as if he might be able to solve a riddle. As if he had a sin to confess.

They're sitting in another part of the island, the site of Hélène's childhood picnics, and she is still trying to find out what Marie-Pierre Sauvé was like before she died.

She seemed nice, he giggled. That's all Thomas can say about her.

"Did you talk to her very much?"

"Why do you ask me that?"

Hélène shrugs.

"It makes her more real."

"That's sick!"

He pulls out small tufts of grass around him.

"That's really sick!"

"I know."

Children are playing ball not far away. Hélène watches them. Then she turns her gaze towards the river.

"I don't understand. What did she do to tolerate it?"

"She's dead too!" says Thomas.

"Yes, but what about before? What happens before? It's like a baby who's being battered to death. How can he tolerate what goes on before he dies?"

"Maybe he passes out."

Hélène gives Thomas a look at once pleading and grateful. She hadn't thought of this; that's right, she passed out. There's a limit to suffering which no one goes beyond.

That notion gives her such relief she starts to cry. All the rest that's been waiting inside her brain for so long before emerging, exploding, soiling the entire universe, the rest that is the suffering borne by thousands of the dead, the savagely dead, all that recedes suddenly, it doesn't happen, and she starts to cry.

"Stop! Stop!" says Thomas.

He puts his arms around her. She's all stiff. He strokes her hair.

"I'm stopping," she says, pushing him away.

In Thomas's room a few days later, Hélène is floating above her own body.

So these things still happen this way.

It's rather dark: a child's nightlight is on. Hélène can see her shadow and Thomas's moving on the wall. A shadow theatre, she thinks. She lifts her arm, and a form appears just above Thomas's shoulders. A moment's respite, much too furtive.

She wishes she could stop constantly thinking about something else. But her body is rooted there on the bed.

Actually the blanket is all crumpled under her and gathered into a heap, and Hélène would like to get up and straighten it. Obsessively almost, she'd like to run her hand over it again and again to smooth out the creases. She'd like to go back to her own room where everything is clean and leave her body here in Thomas's room, where she is lying beside him, so close that his skin sticks to hers.

It's hot. Thomas never opens the window wide enough. Maybe it's intentional. Maybe he wants her to feel stifled next to him, wants to feel that she's hot, wants his hands to glide over her skin.

But Hélène doesn't want him to touch or see even a single drop of sweat on her body.

That's just one of the reasons why she is so tense; she's holding back whatever might emerge from her. She purses her lips, above all he mustn't hear the slightest moan from her.

What she can do then is to float above that stiff body, that body which is far too present and that doesn't get anywhere.

It ought to be light and simple as in a waking dream.

It's muggy and complicated, as in a dream where she is suffocating inside an endless tunnel.

Thomas should have jumped on her the other night on the island. She'd have been forced to say yes, to submit to a kind of blind, benevolent determination, and they could have done what hundreds before them have done on the island, with their eyes focused on the leaves of the trees. A part of each of them could then have escaped through the sky. The other part would have joined the earth, roots.

But Thomas didn't do that.

Thomas waited for her to make up her mind and to make the first move that brought them here, to this bedroom within four walls.

She mustn't think about so many things.

For example, she mustn't listen so carefully to the singer who's howling right now. Thomas put on the disk when he came in, it's a habit; for him it's just background noise. But music also has the power to intensify an emotion, and Hélène has to pay attention, she mustn't try to make out the lyrics, she mustn't try to translate them one by one.

Don't sing in your head like that. As if you were alone.

Thomas's hand caresses her all over and she has to concentrate very hard on his hand on her skin so she can feel it.

It's nice sometimes, said a girl in her class.

Don't think about the girls in your class.

Soon, in a few minutes, it will be done, once and for all and forever.

Don't think like that.

You like Thomas's hand. His mouth is moving all over you. You like it that he's breathing faster as if he were inhaling and exhaling his own desire.

What he wants, after all, is to be there, entirely exposed to need, to appetite, and to do what he's doing. He kisses her as he flattens his belly onto hers.

Her belly, her hips, her breasts.

If she stopped thinking altogether, then objects, books, the bed might also start to float. Everything could disappear. Except their bodies.

She has to do certain things. Surely it's her turn, as in a choreography, a *kata*, an exchange of blows. But she doesn't know what they are. She thrusts her pelvis upwards so he can flatten himself against her again.

She wishes she were stronger than he is so she could direct him. She can't. She has no power over him and he has none over her.

They are simply there, doing this thing to get it over with.

But is that the exact truth?

At this very second, Thomas's vision is cloudy and he tells her he loves her.

Why did he have to say that?

The music has to stop.

"Turn off the music," she whispers in his ear.

He thinks it's a declaration of love even though it's an order. He thinks that she wants to plunge them into the purest silence.

A lie, Hélène repeats to herself.

She took off her clothes herself.

There: it's the body of another woman.

The body of another woman with legs spread to make room for the one who loves.

And so everything must result from her will.

She thrusts her pelvis upwards, draws Thomas's to her.

When he starts to enter her, she sees that his eyes are closed, that he's not looking at her. She couldn't stand that.

Her own eyes are open, they have to be if she wants to stay in control and to sense the island, the wind, the leaves of the trees.

Except that Thomas is hurting her.

Except that she is sinking into the mattress and that it doesn't stop hurting.

Should she move?

Talk?

She doesn't know.

And Thomas doesn't know anything either, surely he doesn't know anything. Maybe he doesn't even know what he's doing.

Everything is so heavy. The trees disappeare quickly and Hélène sees herself under the wheels of a truck.

That's not it.

She feels what is entering her and imagines what there is inside her body. She sees walls that are somewhat red and glistening. The core of herself throbs and stretches like the bottom of a cave. And what if there's no end? If it doesn't stop? She sees what there is beneath the surface of her belly, the layers of epidermis, muscles, nerves, and all those organs that function, that meander and move so close to one another. Such proximity! Just there, under her skin! Such confusion! It makes her want to vomit.

But she stays frozen under Thomas.

That's not it.

There must be something besides this rigid moment, crystallized in shame.

Maybe they didn't drink enough.

Maybe by losing her memory.

She waits for it all to be finished, for him to withdraw and roll onto his side.

Then she gets up, dresses without a word. Rushes home.

A shower.

The pain that drains away with the tap water.

It's done.

It's settled, she thinks.

A kind of peace.

Once again, reality has proved her right.

Eight

THE ATTIC

"It's like Thomas's room," Hélène tells Lisa.

"How?"

"Stifling. Full of disordered thoughts."

Lisa is open-mouthed before the image that her sister has just revealed. She lets it turn around in her head for long seconds before she gives her opinion.

"That's because you're too down-to-earth."

Obviously, she'll never be able to understand Hélène. How can she compare an experience like that with a bedroom? For her, the fact that it's a human experience ought to make the thing much more acceptable. It ought to take them away from the horrible animal world.

"Did he tell you he loved you?"

"What do you think?"

"He did?"

"Sure. He couldn't help himself!"

"Lucky you!"

These words might perhaps take Lisa far beyond any bedroom. If he said that he loved her, the rest — the body, the bedroom, the fear — shouldn't have the same importance. She still believes. She believes all the more when she looks at Hélène, at her two feet planted firmly in the ground.

"If somebody loved me," declares Lisa, "I'd go away with him."

An hour later, Hélène leaves the house, still trying to be reasonable: there's no use talking about it. If she mentioned the pain, Lisa could start believing in the need for pain. She'd think it was a way of approaching purity.

When you hurt, it means that you're triumphant. Hélène heard a girl her age say that on the radio. The girl had stopped eating. She was sometimes thrilled to feel her own saliva burning her stomach.

But what Hélène feels is her own inner dryness. No purity. No beyond. Just a part of herself, cruel and dry, against which she can never stop fighting.

That cruel part told Thomas: I don't want to talk to you.

He phoned twice last night, then again this morning, and she told him once more: I don't want to talk to you. Urge to burst into a big laugh filled with the tinkling of bells. It's still better than dying of shame. Still better than having to apologize.

I took off like a thief, she snickers.

And so in one shot she drives away Thomas's cloudy gaze.

There's just one brief item in today's paper, as if the reality of this story had thinned down over the weeks to the point where it now amounted to nothing more than two or three lines at the bottom of the page. Police are continuing their investigation. That's all.

So now that the newspapers have forgotten Marie-Pierre Sauvé, now that even José has stopped talking about her, it is Hélène who must remain vigilant. She believes that this event has roots no one would have suspected.

Here in the garage, for instance, all the customers, men of course, even — why not? — her own father can still be regarded as suspects.

She washes windshields, checks oil, and practises noting mentally certain licence numbers. She remembers the numbers in particular. Numbers are so real; they line up in even, symmetrical columns, ranking themselves on their own, in her head. They dangle the prospect of a possible world that is perfectly ordered.

The day passes before her like a blast of wind.

There's been a change, she thinks sometimes, and she has the impression that she's waking in fits and starts from a long, dreamless night.

That's what you were hoping for.

And so, in the end, our wishes always come true!

"He phoned," Lisa tells her, in secret, when she comes home from the garage.

"Who?"

"Your lover."

Lisa tried unsuccessfully to imagine Hélène with her lover. Just saying that word, lover, seems so eccentric. To her, she's now positive, there's no risk of that happening.

"If you tell mom, I'll kill you," says Hélène.

"Why would I do that?"

"To get revenge."

"What for?"

"For leaving you here alone with Samuel this summer."

"How stupid do you think I am?"

Lisa is well aware of the commotion that would be set off if she told Viviane. Because her little girls wouldn't behave like the others, would they? Not so young! They've been warned so often. So much trouble could be waiting for them at the turning point. They wouldn't do it. It's impossible that they would do it. But Viviane doesn't know that her little girls have some surprises in store for her. Especially her, Lisa. In fact isn't it the only reasonable way to anticipate the future: an unforeseen destiny, a destiny that no one in the house would even think of?

"You have to call him back," she went on.

"I do? Why?"

"Because he sounded worried."

Hélène's hands begin to move. A moment later she makes them disappear under her thighs.

"Mind your own business."

What do I know about Thomas? Hélène wonders once she's alone in her room.

He's like no one else. Not like Martin or her father. No one.

He would be capable of fighting for an idea. But he could never defend her, Hélène. It would be too easy for her to drag him to the depths of her fear.

That is what she knows.

But Hélène does not know, will never know how he felt once he was inside her, his arms folded along her body. What vision passed before his eyes. Unless for him that moment was completely devoid of vision.

Hélène, in contrast, understood at once what she was already afraid of: her body had closed like a metal box. That's how it is. For how else could she deliver the surface and then the contents of that so imperfect body to another person's gaze?

Huge posters on walls, love scenes in movies, exchanges in magazines . . . None of that is true, those bodies don't have viscera, they haven't surrendered themselves, and never again will they be able to tell her what to do. She may have failed that final examination, but failure will never threaten her again. She feels relieved.

The afternoon is drawing to an end; she hears her mother giving orders to the workman who's going to bring the attic back to life. Viviane herself would never say that she gives orders, but that's what she is doing in her falsely simpering voice, and Hélène realizes that doing so gives her intense pleasure.

Nothing ever takes a long time with her mother: the work is already underway.

"Construction can go very quickly," she told Hélène, to reassure her.

"Destruction goes even faster," Hélène added promptly.

Hammer blows will start raining down as early as eight A.M. tomorrow and the whole family will finally have good reasons to feel an unforgivable urge to run away.

That's what Hélène would like, to find a reason to run away.

She comes out of her room and goes into her parents'. Briefly she studies her own gilt-framed photo sitting on the chest of drawers. Then she parks herself on the bed, tucks her hair behind her right ear, and picks up the phone to call Thomas.

ക

She is sitting on a swing in the park, her outstretched legs gripping Thomas who is standing in front of her. She's almost happy.

Thomas has followed her here, waiting till she decides to talk.

But why would she talk?

About what?

She has talked too often, said too much at times, and today she needs to be silent. To be silent or talk nonsense.

Samuel has come with them, he's there just in front of them in the sandbox. He's playing with his invisible monsters.

Hélène watches him.

Then she starts to talk about the dictionary of monsters Samuel has drawn. It's so amazing. She'd like to talk about the amazing things that Samuel does, all of them, rather than talk about that island or that bedroom or her own hasty departure.

What's past is past: Hélène can transform it in a few nights. Yesterday was yesterday, and today she's at the park, accompanied by Thomas and Samuel.

It's windy, she hates the wind, she hates it so much that she can't explain it, but that's something she won't tell Thomas. Nothing of what could quietly put them back on their own trails, none of that will filter through her words.

Thomas is patient; he doesn't complain. He is waiting for a sign of weakness to escape from Hélène. With her, he now has proof of it, it's impossible to avoid disaster.

But Hélène still says nothing.

She pushes Thomas away, mischievously, and goes over to Samuel.

He stops playing.

"Do you think there's a monster in the river?"

"You mean like the one in Loch Ness?"

"Yes. Do you think so?"

"The river's too small."

"Too small for a monster?"

"There aren't any."

"Yes, but what if there were?"

"If there is one, we'll smash it to death with an axe, okay?"

"Okay."

Hélène looks at Thomas and bursts out laughing.

He grabs her arm.

"That's a stupid thing to say to a child."

"He's not a child, he's my brother."

"Whatever, it's still stupid."

She shrugs. He can provoke her all he wants, he won't get anything from her.

"We have to talk," he goes on.

She hasn't heard a word.

She picks up Samuel's toys one by one. He immediately starts yelling that he can't leave so soon.

"There's a storm coming," says Hélène in a low voice. So low that it surprises even Thomas.

"Are you sure?" asks Samuel.

"Sure I'm sure," she replies.

Thomas is suddenly overwhelmed by the feeling that he doesn't belong here. His big body is standing in a park for children, standing for no reason, and he doesn't know what he's doing here.

"Will you walk us home?" Hélène asks him.

He shakes his head.

She goes up to him, stands on tiptoe and gives him a kiss on the cheek.

"Say bye-bye to Thomas," she tells Samuel.

⚜

It's the same every time for Hélène and Thomas; she wants him to be there, but as soon as he is, she wants him to go away.

"It's terrible when somebody knows too much about you," she tells Lisa.

Lisa certainly doesn't share that opinion. Besides, what is there about Hélène for Thomas to know so well?

"Lots of things," she replies.

"Think about dad and mom!"

"Horrible," says Hélène. "They know so much they don't have anything to say to each other."

One night she dreamed about Thomas. He was sitting on a park bench and crying. It was in Raimbault Park, a magical park with willows bending over a stream. Thomas, wearing clothes that were too big and too black, crying on the park bench, formed a sort of indecent stain in that so-perfect setting.

Maybe he really is unhappy, she thought when she got up this morning.

In fact she knows it: it's she who makes him unhappy. But the question of loving has never come up. Not him and not anyone else.

126

If it were Martin, he'd get angry, Hélène is sure of that. His muscles would tighten. He wouldn't stand frozen there in front of her. His muscles are used to it, they would tighten.

But Thomas is too young for her.

Even if she has to stand on tiptoe to kiss him, she's too big for him.

He's in the kitchen with her. Samuel is finally about to show him his dictionary of monsters.

Viviane has just come in. She makes a face: there's still a lot of noise from the attic.

"Houses aren't selling," she says, setting her purse on the table. It has become a ritual remark.

The year 1994 could be marked in the album of family memories like this: the year when houses stopped selling, the year when the attic was converted.

As soon as she spots Thomas, Viviane offers him something to drink in a burst of exaggerated politeness. Then she unrolls her plans in front of him.

"Do you think he's interested in that?" Hélène grumbles as she leaves the kitchen.

She can't stand to see her mother happy whenever Thomas is there. What difference does it make to her? Why is she always so obviously relieved to see him?

Thomas looks at the plans, unsure of what to say. Fortunately, Samuel mounts a fresh attack with his dictionary.

"This one's always got his mouth open," he explains.

"And this one?"

"He's blind."

Samuel's monsters all have the long bodies of dinosaurs and

long heads like birds. Thomas thinks the dictionary is fantastic. Samuel, terribly proud, runs to tell Hélène.

She's in the chaise longue at the back of the yard, as far from the din as possible.

"You left me all by myself," says Thomas, laughing behind Samuel.

Hélène shrugs.

"My mother's there!" she says.

"That's just it."

Thomas would like to sit next to Hélène but Samuel hasn't finished with him yet. He holds out a ball. Thomas can't resist.

No one can resist Samuel, thinks Hélène. The thought reassures her. Samuel may be the only one here who'll live a normal life.

She watches him playing with Thomas and wonders what he'll do when she's no longer there.

Now he's laughing so hard. And Thomas is having fun too, like a child. Seeing him with Samuel like this, she could almost love him!

Enough! Hélène has had enough of this comedy. She jumps up as if she has just spotted some ferocious animal. The presence of the others weighs her down and she'd like to fling them all to the bottom of a precipice. Let them disappear instantly from her sight!

"We're going inside," she nearly yells to Thomas.

He and Samuel exchange a look, feigning surprise. Then they follow her meekly to the kitchen.

Hélène is silent: this complicity only irritates her some more.

In the house, silence has been restored.

Robert comes home and shortly afterwards, Viviane calls them all for supper.

Lisa comes back from who knows where and sits down without a word. She smiles sadly at Thomas.

Hélène continues to be silent.

At the end of the meal she opens her mouth.

"Well, we won't be dying here tonight."

She takes her jacket and leaves the house. Thomas follows her, happy in turn to go out.

♔

Viviane has to stay home as much as possible to supervise the work. Someone has to be there and Robert stubbornly refuses to help out. In any case, why bother going to the office? She isn't selling anything and she'll soon have to look for a new job.

Humming, Viviane goes up the makeshift stairs to the attic: the transformation is beginning to show. She goes up there with the impression that she's climbing towards the figurative sense of her freedom. She looks up at the ceiling, tries to picture the decorative beam that will soon be placed there. The moment when she'll be able to sit down, alone at last, in this all-white space will be a moment of redemption. A well-earned rest.

"I'm going up to heaven," she sometimes tells her daughters to let them know that she's going to check on the work.

The girls aren't fooled, their mother's joy is always provisional. Above all, it's never infectious.

Lisa is bothered so much by the noise and by the workman's presence that she now spends the better part of her days outside.

"There's nothing to be afraid of," her mother tells her. "I know him well."

Lisa corrects her: she's not afraid, why would she be? She just feels a little uneasy.

She wants to know when the work will be done.

"Soon. After he puts up the beam."

Viviane asks her what she does all day long. Lisa shrugs, irritated. Replies that she doesn't do anything.

Viviane isn't surprised. Lisa has always been a contemplative, secretive child, the very opposite of the other two.

Lisa says: "I try to go to heaven too."

Her mother winks at her, laughing.

Most often, Viviane begs Lisa to take Samuel with her. She adds, always with a smile, not to go too far away. It's a reminder of the memorable time when Lisa came home from the park without Samuel. She'd forgotten him. Quite simply.

Now, though, Samuel is a big boy and there's no danger that he'd let himself be forgotten.

Lisa sits on a park bench, like Thomas in Hélène's dream. But she isn't crying. She is watching the leaves move on the trees. She opens each of the library books she's just taken out. Or she writes a letter to Florence. The children's laughter calmly fades away. Everything is behind her, in a single cloud that she allows to drift away until Samuel tugs on her arm and brings her back to earth.

One afternoon, Lisa comes to see Hélène at the garage. Samuel trots along behind her. All three are standing, leaning against the wall in the body shop.

Samuel watches avidly everything that's going on inside. For the time being, his sisters' conversation doesn't interest him.

"Do you think dad's going to leave again?" Hélène asks Lisa.

"Why ask me?"

"Because."

"I know. Because of the attic."

Lisa too remembers very well the time when Robert packed his bags: it was the last day of the work in the kitchen. The house had been in constant turmoil for more than three weeks, then everything had stopped dead: Viviane couldn't make up her mind about certain details. At the end of that day, everything seemed to be running away between her fingers.

There was already a cold war: their paradise had been an armed camp for a long time. And now, suddenly, there was a moment of total silence. As if all the fuses in the house had blown at the same time. A crucial stage in their lives had been reached without their knowledge.

"Anyway, as far as I'm concerned it doesn't matter any more," said Lisa.

"Same here," Hélène agrees.

And there they are, starting to list a series of things that are more serious and more important than the possibility that one of their parents will walk out.

The river: it's so polluted.

The fish will disappear, and the eagles, the belugas, the elephants.

Sometimes, in other countries, it's even worse, the rivers are full of blood.

Sometimes, the streets, the houses, even the churches are full of bodies.

All those dead soldiers, all those mass graves.

Famine, disease.

And what happened on the island, behind a church, in a parking lot or at the end of an alley.

And what will happen.

The world is full of morbid promises.

So weighty are earthly matters, so obscure.

Fine.

"But what if he's really unhappy?"

"You mean unhappy enough?"

"Yes."

"Then we'd have to help him leave."

"And mom?"

"Her too."

Samuel turns towards his sisters, stunned for a moment.

There they go again!

They start with a tiny little idea.

And then it grows and spreads like mushrooms.

♔

The closer Thomas gets to Hélène, the more she moves away.

Why is he touching me again?

There are other girls, she tells him softly.

He can't come up with an answer. He'd like to. He'd like it if a grand lesson in courage would dictate the words to him. But it doesn't happen.

Hélène knows she ought to stop calling him.

For a couple of days, she doesn't.

Then he calls her.

She says yes.

Her mother is happy, her father is happy, everyone is waiting for Thomas to come over.

Having Thomas means being a normal girl in a normal family.

At noon the workman now eats with them. That's even better. The family is growing!

"The end is in sight!" Viviane exclaims every evening.

They, the children, can't see. Going up is strictly forbidden.

"Too dangerous," says Viviane.

Robert looks at her. He's even more exasperated by her energy than by her bad moods.

Now Hélène too would like to begin to forget about the corpse found on the island. The young girl's features could be slowly erased. The marks her body left in the mud could be completely covered.

She would stop thinking about the clothes, the teeth, the jewellery, the hair. And about the frozen smile in the photo.

It would be the memory of a distant acquaintance surfacing more and more rarely. Like an injury suffered long ago. The more days passed, the more the memory of that injury would disappear under new images.

She could even, if she wanted to, hide her notebook between two walls in the attic.

Or bury it in the yard.

Or throw it very far away into the river.

But things come back.

The drowned emerge on the other shore.

The ice melts and lets you catch sight of objects that were lost at the beginning of the winter.

Rain scrapes the earth.

The walls of houses crumble.

The secrets of children spring up again.

And so the spirit of the year 1994 might well reveal itself at the most unexpected time and place.

♔

Just as Samuel manages to take her hand, her father leaves the earth and flies away slowly into the sky.

"Like a fish," says Samuel.

"You mean like a bird that flies?"

"No, like a fish that slides."

"That's an incredible dream," says Lisa.

Suddenly she can no longer hear the power drill or the voice of her mother chatting outside with the neighbour, or the voice of Hélène who is arguing with Thomas on the phone. She can't hear anything at all.

This is the last time, says Hélène, hanging up.

She goes up to her room, pulls on her jeans that are torn at the knees and her black T-shirt, pulls her hair back as tightly as she can.

She thinks again about the jotting in her notebook: *a black T-shirt with Converse on the front.* The letters leap before her eyes like blinking lights, then are extinguished at once.

When she arrives at the garage José is already there, talking with Émile.

Hélène observes him from a distance. He's making her more and more uncomfortable.

She imagines him guilty of murder, handcuffed, flanked by two policemen, an idiotic smile on his lips, and she sees herself out of range, smashing his car windows with a rod.

She's angry at herself.

So worried.

All day, she keeps an eye on the comings and goings on the street.

Something is going to happen, something is about to occur.

When she spies Thomas coming towards her, her anger is let loose, leaving her only a single dot of pain.

On the way home, she stops abruptly and says to Thomas: "What if it were you?"

It takes him a while to understand.

Then it hits him hard, like a punch.

"I was only kidding," Hélène adds quickly when she sees his reaction.

She grabs his arm, insisting: "It was just a joke!"

But Thomas can't understand another word.

An endless pain is flowing in his veins. He forces himself to glimpse a forest, a beach, any place at all that's big enough to get lost in.

He frees his arm, circles Hélène's neck with his hands.

"Leave me alone," he whispers in her ear.

Hélène feels Thomas's hands for long minutes.

She'd like to see two little red marks on her neck.

She runs to the bathroom to look at herself in the mirror, but she sees only smooth, unmarked skin.

Her face is detached from reality, like an old poster peeling off the wall.

Nine

REDEMPTION

*T*oday is the day when the big wooden beam will pass through Viviane's heaven.

Viviane likes things that look old-fashioned. Twenty years ago she chose this house precisely because it was a little dilapidated. That was at the time when she and Robert, a couple, could still imagine a future in the ruins.

This time, she wants the walls in her room painted white, like in a house at the seaside.

When everything is ready, she'll be able to go up there, forget about the river, the children, above all her husband, forget about words and think in the most detached manner possible about what she'll do when the house is completely renovated.

If heaven is up above, hell is down below, says Hélène with a smile. The bedrooms represent purgatory and hell is down below.

"Hell is on earth," she adds.

"The Aztecs," says Lisa, "believed that hell was made up of nine plains."

Hélène pretends to be trying intensely to see what connection there could be with nine plains in the living room, the kitchen, the dining room. But it's so cramped here; nothing resembles a plain.

"It's the number that counts," declares Lisa. "Numbers are always symbols."

Seven murders, nine plains.

"Numbers are numbers," Hélène corrects her.

Building something makes our mother happier than anything we could do, think the children sometimes. Thinks Robert as well, who has started biting his nails.

"Is she going to sleep up there?" Hélène asks him when he puts in an appearance in the house.

"Come off it, Hélène!" he replies.

He seems as annoyed as if she has read right through him.

That's what she was hoping for. For the thread of an idea to pass through him and make him infinitely transparent.

Lisa, curled up in one corner of the living room, has heard nothing.

It's Samuel's turn to think there's a danger threatening him. He's been grumbling over nothing for several days. He slaps himself on the head.

Robert has just noticed it.

"It must be school," declares Hélène.

"That's right, it's school," says Lisa.

Robert goes up to him, but Samuel shows him his fist.

"I want to go to jail."

Robert is dumbfounded.

"What are you talking about, going to jail?"

Samuel looks at Hélène, doing his best to hide his smile. He's aimed right again. Words are so powerful. Even if he risks losing the use of them a little in school, words will always be powerful. That certainty enlightens him a little more every day.

In front of Viviane, who is doing the dishes, Robert wonders again about this jail business.

Viviane shakes a flowered cloth as she says: "I don't have time to get upset."

Robert turns around, muttering: "It's always one of them!"

That's true; when it's not Hélène turn it's Lisa's, or Samuel's. For Robert, it's the revelation of the year: if it's not one, it's the other.

Maybe after all he's the one who ought to sleep in the bedroom at the seaside.

He sees his children again when they were small and wonders quite seriously why they've grown. He thinks in particular about Hélène and Lisa. Certain stages in life don't interest him in the least.

The three children have just spread their school supplies on the living room floor.

Samuel sharpens all his pencils and stows them in the inner pocket of his new schoolbag. The notebooks are placed there in order of size, the way Hélène taught him.

"Are you happy?" she asks him.

"Maybe," he replies.

But a kind of apprehension has lodged inside him and his tummy aches all the time.

"You'll like it, I know you will."

"Anyway," says Lisa to herself, "summer holidays are finally over."

"But there's more than a week left!" says Hélène.

A big week that seems like a precipice; they've prepared themselves too early. They're always ready too long in advance. Ready for the worst, like soldiers in battle position.

"A week! That's nothing!" exclaims Samuel.

"You're right, it's nothing," says Lisa.

She thinks about the summer that has just gone by. So many new thoughts have been born, so many others have died. Seven days is nothing.

An atom of life, thinks Lisa. Like her life. A speck of time that will leave the universe one day.

⚜

No one in the house talks about Thomas any more. Hélène has forbidden it.

She sometimes strokes the skin on her neck, smiling. That moment belongs only to her.

After all, she catches herself thinking, maybe life isn't so dark.

After all, joy may perhaps be able to take over her body.

It will be a raw joy then: a rain of little needles on her skin.

⚜

If I look at things differently, they will be different.
Today is a different day.

Hélène doesn't know why this is happening to her now, but there it is, a burst of excitement for no reason breathes complete sentences into her head. It must be because of the autumn, which will soon be here.

Today, for instance, she can hear the trees talking to her. The roots that feed them, the branches that soar up towards the sky. They're magnificent right now, at the end of summer.

The island is magnificent too, and will be more and more throughout the month of September. That's what her father has always said: September is the most beautiful month of the year. It's also the month when she was born. And Samuel.

Her birth. And what if she had really managed to become another as she'd hoped so much at the beginning of the summer?

Maybe she really did want to become nobody, like a tree, and maybe she has just arrived there, a tree among the trees, a body among the bodies.

Then that would explain this moment of exaltation.

She has of course learned to feel a secret pain, but isn't that just the beginning of her transformation?

After all, life may not be so dark.

Surely no darker than the bottom of the river, which is black, of course, but which contains nothing but sludge, mud, mud that's alive as in any other river.

No doubt she'd only have to look at the river differently for it finally to stop attracting her towards the bottom.

She would just have to see each thing differently.

The murder, for instance, she'd have to see it as an isolated event. Thomas told her that a thousand times. But how could she listen to him when her own murdered ghost, her other self, kept coming back to her constantly?

Summer is ending and they haven't found anything, José will say once again, today. The murderer will never be arrested. But maybe he's dead too? Or he's waiting for winter to kill again and this time he'll leave stockings on his victim. Hélène knows that one murderer who is still free has behaved that way. He'll take pity on his victim and want to warm her feet before he kills her. An act of contrition. Maybe. Whatever.

But she, Hélène, will soon have to stop imagining.

One of these days she'll have to decide to throw away her notebook before everything ends up really badly. Before Samuel and Lisa find it, for instance, and death settles into the house for good.

Another year is opening to her and, in a sense, she has taken her obsession to its logical conclusion. Maybe that means there is an end for everything?

She has also experienced love, which for her was non-love.

It's normal at my age, she thinks with exaggerated off-handedness.

Normal, like growing up in a house filled with hidden possibilities, like temporary possibilities — a pounding heart, terror.

If you look at life differently, everything can of course slip into the ordinary world. That's the way it is. The world of trees. The world of bodies rotting in the earth. The world of oblivion.

So there is one day like that, and then another. A sort of temporary respite, a valley where Hélène stops to catch her breath. And then it's the whole neighbourhood that seems to be resting.

No one could believe in fact that a murderous tremor has already shaken the island, the streets, the houses.

It's so peaceful.

Are all the children at this very moment busy counting the days like Samuel? Although Hélène tells him precisely how many days, hours, minutes, never will he understand what it means. Hélène knows full well that these holidays haven't been what they should have been for him and even more for Lisa. She thinks that she's somewhat responsible.

Today though she wants to step across the footbridge that leads her to another part of herself, to a part that is irresponsible, moveable, hazy; and if she does that, even if it only lasts for one day, Samuel and Lisa can also go on doing it.

They have to, thinks Hélène.

A hint of anxiety that she kills off by blinking her eyes.

And what if they should take the opposite road?

⚜

The hours go by, quick and luminous as fireflies.

Lisa too is preparing for the arrival of another season. She has restored order to her room, thrown several old things into a big bag. Then she got her hair cut.

She walked into the hairdressing salon shyly; she took a photo of an actress from her pocket.

"It's good to start the year with a new look," said the hairdresser when he'd nearly finished the cut.

She looked for a long time at her wavy hair that lay at her feet, forming a kind of crown.

As she shut the door of the salon, she started on her destiny: to be as free as a flag flying very high in the wind.

At first Viviane and Robert are outraged, mainly because she did it without asking their opinion.

Hélène comes to her sister's defence: "It's her hair!"

Then they feel relieved: Lisa is getting ready for school, she's better now, soon order will be restored.

Hélène looks at Lisa and thinks for a moment.

"Now you look even more like an angel."

"An angel face," says Lisa later, as she studies her reflection in the mirror. As if it were possible to make what you want to be inside coincide with what appears on the outside!

Wings grow inside, not outside, thinks Lisa.

Not outside.

She smiles. That thought is absolutely intoxicating.

Wings grow, they take over the heart and the mind, they finally cast a shadow on the body, on the present, the future, on words, matter — on every object that constitutes chaos.

⚜

Lisa's new hairdo has made concrete Samuel's feeling of insecurity.

"There are three days left," Hélène has told him.

This time, he understood. He got up in the middle of the night to vomit.

"It's just a tiny little change," Hélène explains to him.

The din from the attic is infernal and she practically has to shout.

"Just a little longer than kindergarten."

But Samuel won't accept any explanation.

"You don't understand," he tells her.

Hélène is a little surprised: understand what?

"But school is fun, you're going to learn how to read!" she tells him, trying with all her might to convince herself. Also.

"You don't understand."

In the house, the change becomes perceptible for everyone as soon as silence pushes open the door to resume its place. The place for the new beginning isn't finished yet. Something has changed, but no one knows what. Hell is made up of plains that are too peaceful.

Down below, Robert and Viviane might very well start talking.

Up above, in his room, Samuel draws monsters and handcuffs with a lingering aftertaste in his mouth.

Lisa observes the river through the window.

There is that August wind, a movement in the leaves that's nearly cold, a movement on the surface of the water that's a harbinger of what's to come.

Hélène unlocks her drawer, this time determined to erase everything.

⚜

Saturday.

Hélène left the house early that morning for her last day at the garage.

Huguette has offered to let her go on working weekends, but Hélène said no.

She'll miss the garage. The smell, the pumps, the mechanics of her own movements. For the first time, she's going to miss something.

She waits feverishly for customers to arrive. Every time one of them leaves, she feels as if she is drawing a line through one part of her life.

At noon she goes home to eat. She wolfs down a sandwich in company with Samuel, Robert, and Viviane. Lisa is still in her room.

"She's already eaten," says Viviane, her voice slightly strained.

When the meal is over, Lisa emerges from her room and sits down next to Hélène. She looks at her in silence.

"What's the matter?" Hélène asks her.

"Nothing," Lisa replies. "I just wanted to see you before you left."

She runs her hand through her hair.

"You're out of it again!" says Hélène.

They get up and go outside to join the others.

Samuel is already catching ants that he'll put in his insect jar. Viviane has just stretched out on the deck to read the paper and Robert is finally doing something in the garden. Now Lisa settles onto a chaise longue.

Hélène observes them, trying to figure out what's wrong with this picture formed by her family. She shrugs.

"Okay, I won't bother you any more!" she tells them as she walks away.

At the garage, she thinks about Thomas. Then about Martin.

She wants to go back to the club after work. It's not a desire, not even a need; she sees herself quite simply going in, saying hi to Martin, and apologizing for her madness at the beginning of the summer, as if that madness were suddenly and permanently over. She also sees herself creasing her eyes, preferring not to look around too much in case her mind should give out on her again. Because she never knows when the blackness of the river will come back up to her.

She'll go to the club then, at the end of the afternoon, and instantly regain that impression of fraternity, of protection, of abduction. But not shame, no, there won't be any more shame.

That's all over and done with, she thinks.

After that she tries to imagine the day of her birthday, which will soon be there. A party is unfolding just for her, like a peacock's tail. But even in her dreams she can't believe in it.

She opens the door to the boxing club for the second time. And at that very moment, in reality, she spots Samuel. He's running towards her like a little bird that's going to crash into a window.

It's impossible to know what's going on: Samuel's voice is shaken by hiccups. He ran too fast, holding back the sobs that are now rushing out of him.

"What is it, Samuel?" Hélène keeps repeating.

"Let him catch his breath," says Huguette.

But Hélène can't stop: she feels as if she's falling into a bottomless well.

The river where someone is in the process of drowning.

The security perimeter that people now set up around their own houses.

What has happened to Samuel?

"What's wrong, Samuel?" she asks again.

She shakes him by the shoulders.

"What's going on?"

He tries his best to get a grip on himself.

"She cried," he manages to say a moment later.

"Who cried?"

"Mummy."

"Why did she cry?"

"She was in the attic."

"In the attic? But what did she say exactly, Samuel?"

"Go away, Samuel. Get out of the house."

"Why did she say that? Why?"

Samuel starts to cry again.

Then Huguette gestures to Hélène to stop asking him questions.

"We'll go back to the house," she tells them. "It can't be anything serious."

The three of them walk in silence. Viviane's cry is still echoing in Samuel's ears.

He doesn't understand.

Then the cry awakens in his brain. It was Lisa's name.

It was Lisa's name that his mother screamed before she cried out his name.

On Saint-Réal Street, at the end of the blind alley, they see the ambulance, the rotating lights, the neighbours, and Robert and Viviane. Their movements are vague and dislocated, as in a nightmare.

"It's Lisa," says Samuel finally.

⚜

Something has happened, something has finally happened.

It's Lisa, Samuel's voice repeats in Hélène's head.

Viviane has found Lisa.

She saw her feet, and after that she saw her body, and after that her face, and then, after some interminable seconds of madness, she must have know that it was Lisa; it entered her awareness like an electrical shock, a volley of shot piercing her body, covering her with powder, ash, dust, and then she had to know what it was. She had to tell Hélène, and then Samuel. Lisa has hanged herself from the beam.

Hanged, that word alone can now demolish everything Hélène
has learned, heard, understood in the course of her life.

Hanged, like the prisoner in the dome, like all those who hang
themselves with a rope.

She made the knot, she pushed away the chair. Lisa?

That's impossible. A secret that's too powerful.

Not here. Not in a house. Not on the earth.

Not Lisa.

⚜

A shipwreck with survivors. An old image of a boat sinking
into the sea of darkness: lethal waves submerging the decks,
outstretched arms escaping from the eddies. Flesh-eating survivors.
Survivors in search of the secret slowly losing their minds.

Hélène wishes she could cry out into her parents' faces disfigured
by their inability to comprehend: Lisa wasn't Lisa.

Lightness, secret, sacrifice.

And me, I'm not myself.

She asks them where they were when Lisa . . . Even if she
knows, she asks again. And again.

They'd gone out with Samuel to do their shopping.

What, all three of them? That's absurd. Absurd, Hélène repeats
over and over.

But the outing had been planned for several days. Hélène
knew that.

Lisa did too and at the last minute, she flatly refused to go.
Nearly the first signs of anger.

What's got into her today? Robert had wondered.

Viviane and Samuel came home first. Two hours later. Their

arms full of bags.

And then Robert: he'd forgotten to buy something.

Right away he heard Viviane's sobs coming from the attic. They seemed to be coming from a person he didn't recognize.

It was he who took Lisa down.

One second later, his whole life was spread on the ground, the empty places, the full ones, love in small doses, and he in turn started to cry.

The explosion of such cries in the house of silence.

It should have been me, Hélène would like to say.

For the rest of her life, the rest of the days and nights, the rest of the evenings sitting on the bank of the river, in a house that is more and more empty, she will know: what was burning inside her had finally perhaps touched Lisa. But it should have been her. Hanged. Buried. Forgotten as a person.

She looks at her parents sitting in the living room: they're unreal. What will happen now? What will the world be like for Samuel?

She hears the attic breathing above her.

She arranges flowers in a vase. Then goes upstairs.

Caught by the waves of light, she sets the vase on the floor and sits on the chair.

She searches her sister's room, following Viviane and Robert, but there's nothing. No sign. Not even the slightest trace of the letters signed by Florence. Lisa took care to erase everything.

She searches again, from top to bottom.

Then she remembers: for Lisa, the reasons for existing, or the non-reasons, always illuminate us from the inside.

On earth, there is hell. In heaven, light.

Lisa's non-reason has been extinguished with her.

One day, there's a call from Florence. Hélène answers. Half an hour later, she hangs up.

She sits at the kitchen table. She sees Lisa's feet appear.

She stops crying.

She sometimes thinks back to the details that reveal human monstrosity, but her locked drawer stays empty. No more notebook, no more wedding photo. Nothing.

She woke up Samuel this morning, saying: this time, we have to go.

They are on the boulevard.

The brand new schoolbag is huge on Samuel's bent back. At every corner, Hélène stops to reassure him. He smiles at her. She sees their shadows lengthening on the sidewalk.

She leaves Samuel in the hands of his new teacher, certain that he'll be better off at school than in the house which now belongs to Lisa's death, to Viviane's cry, and Robert's.

If I'd done it, she thinks, I'd have chosen blood.

But she has stayed behind in the world. Alive.